SOLO

PRIMAL SIN #3.5

ARIANA NASH

Solo, Primal Sin #3.5

Ariana Nash - *Dark Fantasy Author*

Subscribe to Ariana's mailing list & get the exclusive story 'Sealed with a Kiss' free.

Join the Ariana Nash Facebook group for all the news, as it happens.

Copyright © June 2022 Ariana Nash

Edited by Sue Laybourn / Proofreader Jennifer Griffin

Warning: The unauthorized reproduction or distribution of this copyrighted work is illegal. Criminal copyright infringement, including infringement without monetary gain, is investigated by the FBI and is punishable by up to five years in federal prison and a fine of $250,000.

Please note: Crazy Ace Publishing monitors international pirate sites for infringing material. If infringement is found (illegal downloading or uploading of works) legal action will be taken.

US Edition. All rights reserved.

No part of this book may be reproduced in any form or by any electronic or mechanical means, including information storage and retrieval systems, without written permission from the author, except for the use of brief quotations in a book review.

All characters and events in this publication, other than those clearly in the public domain, are fictions, and any resemblance to real persons, living or dead, is purely coincidental.

Edited in US English.

Version 1 - June 2022

www.ariananashbooks.com

CHAPTER 1

*S*olo

SOLO DID NOT BEGRUDGE his duty ensuring ex-High Lord Luxen and his cohort Samiel were safely confined in the exotic animal enclosures in a repurposed area of an old abandoned zoo.

Luxen had schemed his way into being High Lord of the demons, and plotted multiple ways to kill—and when that hadn't worked, seduced—Mikhail, and Samiel had aided and abetted the High Lord for years. There could be no doubt as to their guilt. Mikhail had entrusted Solo with their incarceration. However, Solo *did* begrudge how the mere sound of Lord Luxen's smooth, deep demon voice writhed its way under his skin to seemingly take control of his body. Especially the male appendage he'd discovered had a more pleasurable use beyond expelling unwanted bodily fluids.

Things had been far more straightforward when his male member hadn't had a mind of its own. Now, when he visited Luxen and Samiel, within a few minutes his mind was split between his duty and the undeniable urge to stare at Lord Luxen's ripped physique. Luxen knew it too, of course. The demon lord's gaze set Solo's red wings ruffling, as it seemed as though he could read Solo's mind. Solo had asked Severn (High Lord Konstantin, as most demons knew him) if Luxen had the power to read his mind. Severn had replied that Solo might not be too difficult to read, and he should avoid Luxen's gaze.

But that was easier said than done. Where else was Solo supposed to look? In the hot enclosure, the demon was always shirtless. There were only a few places to observe his body without accidentally gazing at a nipple or some other tantalizing piece of him. Like his wings. Solo could most definitely *not* stare at those, with their large canvas of quivering leather and prominent, radiating veins, demanding to be touched.

All concubi demons needed physical contact—or more accurately ether— to survive. Trapping Luxen behind toughened glass was tantamount to torture. But, on the other hand, he had tried to kill Mikhail, so the demon lord deserved his punishment. He'd been... quieter of late. Isolation was clearly wearing on him. Not that Solo cared. It was just he hated to see any creature suffer, even one as dastardly as Luxen.

Perhaps the length of his stay should be brought to an end soon, to lessen his suffering. He'd ask Mikhail...

Solo approached the door leading into the enclosure, these thoughts whirring in his head. So many thoughts about Luxen and the past, the war, and demons, that he almost missed how the main door hung open a crack.

It was supposed to be locked.

Solo's heart lurched. He flung open the door and dashed into the animal enclosure. Luxen was behind his glass, exactly where he was supposed to be, seated on his bench, one leg extended, casual as you like. But the second enclosure, where Samiel had been housed, that door hung wide open. Samiel had escaped.

"Oh no..." He entered Samiel's empty enclosure, not knowing what he expected to find. There were no corners to hide in. Samiel wasn't here. He'd escaped. But how?

The door... Solo examined the lock. Intact. No signs it had been forced. Samiel hadn't broken his way out, someone had *let* him out.

Samiel was free.

Mikhail had to know—*immediately*.

"Angel."

Luxen's drawl slithered down the back of Solo's neck and kept right on going, touching that sensitive spot between his wings. He almost didn't turn. Knew he shouldn't listen. Luxen was everything angelkind feared. He gave demons a bad name. But he must have seen Samiel escape, seen who unlocked the door, could describe them. Might even know where they went.

Solo swallowed and turned to face Luxen. "Who let him out?"

Luxen arched a single eyebrow. "Let who out?"

"Samiel—" Solo pressed his lips together, cutting himself off. Luxen's smirk said he knew who Solo was referring to. Of course he did. Solo stepped closer to the glass. His wings twitched, opening wider, making himself bigger when faced with the enemy. "You saw, didn't you? You saw everything."

"That depends..." The demon pushed from the bench and approached the glass. He walked like a panther—all slinky and slow, as though each of his muscles contained raw power ready to be unleashed. Strong, veined forearms and a powerful chest... and lower, where the plane of his flat stomach dove into a tantalizing V-shape and disappeared behind the waistband of his leather pants. Solo definitely should not be looking there. And not into Luxen's eyes either. Severn had been clear on that. Solo blinked and stared at Luxen's wings instead. Their jagged tips towered, all angles and points, but also smooth, leathery, and strangely featherless.

Since Severn and Mikhail had ended the war, demons lived among angels. Solo saw demon wings most days, but there was something about Luxen's wings that made each of Solo's glossy red feathers stand on-end and shiver.

"Let me go," Luxen purred, "and I'll tell you all I saw."

Solo huffed through his nose. "You think me a fool."

"Now, angel." Luxen braced an arm against the glass. His sly smile grew, revealing just a hint of sharp teeth. "We've been through this. I don't think you a fool. In fact, I'm rather fond of you. Let me go and I promise not to hurt you."

"*You're* the fool if you believe I'd do such a thing." Solo stepped back, tucked his wings in, and lifted his chin. "I don't need your help."

Luxen smiled. "All right. I can see you're an angel of your word. For your kindness and bringing those delicious sandwiches, I'll tell you. Come closer."

The glass between them was three inches thick. Sound

travelled through the holes near the top and bottom, where the glass was fixed into the floor and ceiling. Luxen could not reach Solo.

Solo stepped closer. He'd been visiting Luxen for weeks now. Bringing food. Seeing to his personal welfare needs. He wasn't afraid of the demon. He was afraid of... himself. But he controlled these strange new urges. They did not control him.

"Closer... please. It's not a lot to ask. Unless you're afraid?"

He could not let Luxen see how getting too close set Solo's heart racing. Or how he'd dreamed so many times of unlocking the door, stepping inside, and facing the High Lord with no glass between them. And all the things that happened after that left him waking with his hard member in his hand, the only relief that which he pumped from himself.

He stepped up to the glass, putting him within inches of the formidable demon. Luxen was slimmer than most others of his kind but at least a foot taller than Solo. The horns made him taller still. His deep golden skin shimmered, and the wings... *Don't look into his eyes, don't look into his eyes, don't look into his—* His eyes were beautiful, like an ocean horizon stained by the setting sun. Mostly orange and red, with specs of green and blue. Up close, they were as molten as lava speckled with precious gems. *Mesmerizing.*

"This is what I know, angel," Luxen said so softly he almost whispered. "You will return, you will ask for my help, and in exchange, you will unlock this door, and you and I will—"

Solo snarled and, turning on his heel, he thrust out his

wings as though to flick the demon away with his feathers. "I will *never* set you free."

The High Lord's laugh followed Solo long after he'd left the prison. It echoed through his thoughts and pumped heat through his veins. It was just the maddening urges, just the High Lord's *allure*—a way to get what he wanted from Solo. It wasn't real, and Solo could fight it.

He took to the sky and headed for Aerie's shimmering disks high among the clouds over London—flying hard and fast. Mikhail and Severn must know of Samiel's escape. Nobody was safe until the demon was recaught, especially Severn. Now free, Samiel would want only one thing: revenge.

CHAPTER 2

olo

AERIE WAS awash with chatter and light. The city on stilts high above London had recently been rebuilt, rapidly becoming the central hub for trade and negotiations among angel and demonkind. Enormous glass domes arched over multiple platforms—Aerie's infamous disks—and each one buzzed with activity. Demons and angels gathered in pairs or small groups. Feathered wings ruffled and fluttered. Leathery wings flapped and stretched. The grumble and growl of deep demon voices mingled with the lighter, bubblier, high-pitched angel laughter.

The Aerie Solo had known during the war had been cold, sharp, and unforgiving. Things were changing for the better now demons were among them. But there was still a long way to go, or so Mikhail had confided in Solo. Centuries of war could not be resolved overnight.

Solo landed lightly, tucked his wings in, and strode down the spiral staircase to the council chamber. He interrupted a heated meeting regarding the rejuvenation of Dagenham—demon territory almost decimated by war—and asked for High Lord Konstantin or His Grace Mikhail's whereabouts, as neither were among those gathered. Following the directions relayed, and after some back and forth between Aerie's disks, he found the pair outside one of the eateries, standing close against a balustrade and clearly engrossed in one another. Mikhail's hand rested on Severn's arm. He said something, with his head bent low, and Severn's smile lit his face.

They made a marvelous pair. Severn was huge, his demon skin dark and touched with molten veins. Mikhail was imposing too, in an angel way. His midnight wings framed the dark-haired guardian—the epitome of angel. Solo's heart spluttered at the sight of them. So many complicated emotions raced into his mind. Fate had been cruel to Severn and Mikhail, but they'd survived, and thrived.

Would anyone ever gaze at Solo with the same love and admiration as these two looked at each other? He doubted it, but that was all right. He didn't expect to find a love like theirs. Their love was legendary.

He cleared his throat, closed the last few strides, and dropped to one knee. "Your Grace, High Lord. I come with dire news."

"Solo, please rise," Mikhail said. "We've discussed this. You do not need to kneel."

It was habit, and only right. He rose, straightened, thumped a fist to his chest, opened his mouth to explain how he'd lost Samiel, only to find his voice had abandoned him. How could he tell them both he'd failed so spectacularly in his duty? They looked at him, they waited. Sunlight warmed Severn's impressive horns and kissed every one of Mikhail's velvety black feathers. Happiness radiated from them. Solo's news would ruin this moment. Perhaps Solo could find Samiel, return him to the enclosure, and Mikhail and Severn need never know. Solo was, after all, their appointed General of Aerie's Flights—although those flights had been disbanded since they'd laid down their angelblades on the battlefield.

"Solomon?" Mikhail arched a dark eyebrow. "What is it?"

Severn's eyes narrowed. As concubi, he *could* read Solo's ether. Solo's was probably churning.

Angels did not lie. But he could... delay telling the truth. And if he recaptured Samiel soon, they might never need to know? No harm done.

"It's the cats," Solo blurted, grasping at the most dire thing he could think of. Guilt squirmed inside, making him wish he could begin this entire conversation again. "One is missing." Which was true. The multicolored one with half a tail had not returned that morning. She usually curled up next to Solo on his bed and purred loudly when he woke, but not that morning.

"That's your definition of dire?" Severn said.

"I just... it's... Five." Solo waved a hand. "I'm not sure what I'm supposed to do. Do I look for her, or do I wait for her to return by her own means?"

"*Five* are missing?" Mikhail enquired, his face perplexed.

"No, it's called Five," Severn said. "Remember?"

"Yes." Solo exhaled, relieved they appeared to be on

board with this explanation. Although Severn didn't seem convinced. "There are six. They are each named numbers One to Six, to keep things simple."

"Oh yes, I recall..." Mikhail shared a glance with Severn.

"I would wait a few days," Severn suggested. "And if Five hasn't returned, put up a missing poster, like humans do."

"That's a great idea. Thank you. I'm so relieved. I knew you'd have the answer." He backed away. "Thank you, again. A missing poster. Yes, I'll do that." Solo turned on his heel and walked away from the pair, catching the tail end of Mikhail's comment about never knowing an angel to keep pets.

But Solo didn't really *keep* the cats, they just chose to stay. He didn't understand it either, in truth. But he liked their company. It would be so very lonely in the small house without them.

He marched to the edge of Aerie's disk, spread his wings, and dove over the side. The cool wind pulled him downward, until a warm updraft swirled in, lifting him higher.

He'd almost been caught in a lie. Goodness, whatever was becoming of him? First, he was having *urges* for a demon, and now lies? Is that what emotions did to an angel? No wonder Mikhail had struggled. But he'd had Severn to guide him. Solo didn't have anyone.

A huge shadow swooped down, blocking the sun. Great lava-veined wings flared in front of him. Solo gasped and pulled up, reaching for the angelblade that was no longer at his hip.

Severn saw, frowned, and pointed down, suggesting they land.

Oh no. Severn had seen through the lie. He'd want to know *everything*. Solo sighed, tucked in his wings, and plunged for the nearest rooftop among London's jagged skyline. He landed on a flat roof, startling some roosting pigeons. London was damp and misty, smelling of river and wet concrete. Human sounds bubbled around them. Traffic humming, crossings chiming.

Severn's wings flapped, slowing the demon's bulk, but for all his muscles, he landed as light as a feather. "Now spill it, Solo."

"Spill what?"

"What's going on with you?" Severn grumbled, stalking forward.

"My cat—"

"Really?" Severn snorted. "I'll stop you there before you dig yourself a deeper hole. I know you're lying. I'd know you're lying even if I couldn't read your ether. You're a terrible liar. Most angels are." He held up a hand. "Don't fret, it's a trait. Look, Mikhail bought your story about a cat, but—"

"It's not a story. Five is missing. I didn't lie."

"Then something else is wrong. Mikhail doesn't know, and we can keep it that way, if you want. But you have to tell me or I will tell him something is up with you, and he'll haul your ass back to Aerie and interrogate you until he gets the truth."

Solo chewed on his bottom lip. Perhaps this wasn't so bad. Having Severn know about Samiel's escape meant he could keep Mikhail safe, without Mikhail having to know all the details. "Samiel escaped."

Severn's demon eyes widened. *"What?!"* His growl was so like thunder that Solo almost reached for his blade again. He trusted Severn, he did, it was just... everything was so confusing.

Severn's sail-like wings flared. "How?"

"I... don't know. The enclosures are always locked. Always. I left for a few minutes—not long—to go feed the cats."

Severn pinched the bridge of his nose. His wings drooped. "You do this regularly?"

"Every day. I'm there all night. They can't miss their breakfast."

Severn growled again. "So you routinely leave two extremely dangerous demons without a guard at exactly the same time every day?"

"But not for long, and they can't escape. The enclosures are demon-proof."

"Unless someone has the key."

But Solo had the key. "Well... yes. Clearly."

"Who has access to the key?"

"I er... me." He took the key from his flight jacket pocket and showed it to Severn.

"Are there spares?"

"Yes, I suppose. In Aerie."

"Can anyone in Aerie get the spare key?"

"I... don't think so, no. It's in the armory."

Severn closed his eyes, shook his head, and paced away, just a few strides, then paced back again, wings throbbing with heat. "Please tell me Luxen is still locked up?"

"Yes, he's er... He's still there."

"Well that's something, at least. Samiel is dangerous, definitely, but not like Luxen. Alone, Samiel probably won't do much. He'll go to ground, buy time..." Severn paced some more, then returned again. "Okay, here's what we're going to do. I'm going to go back to Aerie to find out who had access to that spare key. You are going to carry on as though nothing has happened. And we are *not* going to tell Mikhail. He has enough on his mind with the imminent arrival of the European Guardian Angel who is apparently only half-convinced demons have earned their freedom. We need him clearheaded, not worrying about any personal vendetta Samiel has."

"Yes, all right," Solo agreed. "And... I'm sorry. I didn't realize anyone would want to free Samiel. I thought the risk came from within the enclosure, not outside of it."

"Just because we're not openly at war doesn't mean all demons and angels agree with the new way of things. I wish it wasn't like that, but it's too soon for us all to let our guards down."

Solo bowed his head and thumped his chest. "High Lord, forgive me. I will make this right."

"Hey." Severn's heavy hand landed on Solo's shoulder. "Don't worry. We've got this."

"Yes. We have this."

"Good." His wings bloomed behind him. "I'll report back on my findings at sundown." He launched into the air, and within a few superheated wingbeats, vanished into the clouds.

Solo kicked a chunk of brick off the rooftop and watched it plunge to the empty street below. He'd messed up on so many ways. He'd only ever wanted to do good, to do the right thing, especially after learning the right thing hadn't been the right thing at all for most of his life.

Mikhail trusted him. And that was everything. He could not lose his trust.

He had to find Samiel. And fast.

And there was one obvious lead who likely knew exactly where Samiel was; He offered one quick way out of this, a way to make it right.

Luxen.

CHAPTER 3

uxen

THE RED-HAIRED ANGEL named Solomon was a delight to watch as he paced outside Luxen's cell. He'd chosen to wear demon leathers instead of angel armor, and that supple leather hugged Solomon's lithe physique in all the right ways, especially his pert, bitable ass—an ass often hidden by scarlet wings. He strutted in all that leather, wings like warning flags—wings Luxen had to force himself to look away from. They glowed like flames, they were so fine. He ached to touch them. For all the nonsense about demons loving angels and the ridiculous angel allyanse, Luxen hadn't believed it—until this stunning red-haired specimen had blocked his escape moments after Luxen had tried to kill Mikhail and Konstantin.

Solomon, Angel of Aerie.

He'd appeared out of nowhere like a flaming arrow from Seraphim himself and fucked up Luxen's escape plan.

Since then, Luxen hadn't been able to get him out of his head, made worse by the fact Solomon was his jailor too. He brought him dainty sandwiches with the crusts cut off. Once, he'd cut up a radish and crafted it like a rose. Who did that? Solomon, apparently. Did Mikhail know how the sight of this one tormented him? Unlikely. The guardian didn't understand ether. He couldn't. Konstantin then; yes, he'd understand, and if he knew how Luxen craved Solomon's forbidden, untouchable body, he'd make Luxen suffer.

Yes, this was Konstantin's doing.

He hated this angel but also wanted to fuck him.

It was their own doing. Luxen had already been starved of ether for too long. He needed out of this cell, he needed to fuck and feed, and that red-haired angel was his key to freedom. If he'd just agree to free Luxen.

Of course, Solomon would never agree to sex. Not that one. He was far too uptight and repressed. A shame, as the things he could do with that small but powerful body. He'd light the unsuspecting angel on fire. All that passion, that innocence, it made Luxen's concubi heart race and his cock heavy with want. Even now, he was hard. If the angel saw, he'd probably flee. Although, Luxen had seen his curious sideways glances when he thought Luxen's attention was elsewhere. Solomon *was* curious.

The angel suddenly left and with a sigh, Luxen leaned back against the wall and stretched out a leg, alleviating the pressure around his cock. He could will himself hard and soft in a few seconds, but he rather enjoyed the restrained tightness and its demanding ache. He'd imagined all the ways he could have that angel. On his knees, his cock down the angel's throat. Behind him, pounding into his tight, angelic ass while stroking the angel's dick alive and making him scream for more. Luxen would drink him down like the elixir he was, gorge himself on angel, fuck him, bite him, come all over him.

He almost wished he didn't know what angel tasted like. He had Konstantin to thank for that lesson—Severn, as he'd been known then—with his blond hair, fluffy feathers, and a body so starkly contrasting with Luxen's their fucking had almost been poetry.

Luxen hated that he wanted angel. Craved them. Hated how his body sang when he was close to *angel*, especially Solomon. When he was close, Luxen couldn't damn well think of anything else but bedding him.

Solomon returned with a heavy length of chain looped around his arm and wrist shackles in his other hand. *Interesting*.

"All right, demon. This is how it's going to be," Solomon said in his clipped and lofty angel voice. "I am going to let you out to help with finding Samiel, but you will be chained to me the entire time. Do we have a deal?"

Chained to Solomon. *Chained to an angel*. The fool was either mad or ignorant.

Luxen rose from the bench and approached the thick glass. For all his flightiness, Solomon had strength. He had been an impressive warrior, before they'd all given up their swords. Physically, he and this angel were evenly matched. Angels were direct in their attack and defense. If this one was going to attack Luxen, he'd broadcast it in his muscles and wings. But Solomon wouldn't see an attack coming from Luxen, and then there was Luxen's *allure*. Had

Solomon forgotten Luxen had a measure of power over him, a way to tweak his desires, or did he not know? Or perhaps he thought he was strong enough to resist his allure? What a laughable thought that was. Luxen *always* got what he wanted.

"Are you sure?" Luxen asked. "I wouldn't want you to regret your offer."

"I won't regret it." His green eyes sparkled. "I know exactly who—what I'm dealing with." Those lovely eyes flashed with a righteousness angels were notorious for.

"All right. If you think this is the right course of action."

"Step back from the door."

Luxen obeyed, playing the submissive, obedient prisoner. He even let his wings sag, to keep from startling the angel. Solomon took the key from his hip pocket, where not so long ago he'd have worn a sword he'd used for the sole purpose of cutting down demons.

For ten years Luxen had ruled the demonkin. But for a lifetime, he'd watched angels, just like this one, slaughter his kind in their thousands. His earliest memory was of angels tearing his world apart, of dead demons raining from the skies. And now they were supposed to forget all that and just... get along? All the dead, generations wiped out... and he was about to be chained to one of them like an animal on a leash.

The war being over was a convenient excuse for angels to reign over demons. The peace was a sham.

Solo unlocked the door and entered the enclosure. He vanished his wings behind him to keep their fluffy arches from taking up too much room.

"Arm out." He unlopped the length of chain, perhaps

four meters of it. A generous length. More than enough to choke an angel.

Luxen extended his left arm. When a waft of the angel's scent sailed over him, it laced his tongue and tinkled his senses. Solomon smelled of summer meadows, warm and floral. He hadn't expected that, and steeled himself against a brutal surge of desire driven by his starved state. What would Solomon do if Luxen drove him against the enclosure's glass walls and he felt hot, hard demon pressed against him? Would he moan for more or cry for help?

The angel's soft fingers skimmed Luxen's wrist as he clamped the shackle in place, then slotted the lock closed. The touch, so light but precise, struck like lightning. Luxen gritted his teeth.

Solomon took the shackle on the other end of the chain and fumbled it over his right wrist, eventually clamping it closed. He slipped the key to both into that same right-handed pocket. He really wasn't tactically minded. Once Luxen killed him, the key to the cuffs was within easy reach.

Solomon tugged on Luxen's wrist, then his own, testing the shackles' strength. "Now wherever you go, I go."

"And wherever you go, I go."

Solomon's pale face pinched in annoyance. "That's what I said."

"Not really. One of us is free to choose the direction."

"Well, it's implied from the fact we are chained *together*," he said stiffly. He turned and dragged the chain behind him, rattling its many links and making it a few steps before he stooped to scoop up the loose length under his arm.

"A shorter chain might have been more—"

"This was all I could find so this is what I'm using. It's not up for discussion."

Luxen gathered some of the chain's length to keep it from dragging on the floor and followed Solomon from the enclosure. He'd only spent a few weeks locked away but, alone and starving, with just Samiel for conversational company, it had felt like years.

Luxen climbed the steps, out into the open world—in this case, an overgrown abandoned zoo—and a great weight lifted off his shoulders. He spread his wings and gave them a few relieving flicks, then lifted his face to admire the overcast sky. Above those clouds, a long stretch of endless blue beckoned. He wanted to fly almost as much as he wanted to fuck the angel currently staring at him, his green eyes wide in something like wonderment.

Luxen dipped his chin and peered at the angel from the corner of his eye. He angled his wings back, tilting their weight behind him, and sure enough, the angel's gaze followed. It was almost a shame he had to die. He'd have liked to play with this one.

Time to end this.

Luxen tightened his hold on the length of chain, retracted his wings, and jerked the chain, hauling Solomon off-balance and toward him. A punch to the throat would be sufficient—

Cold steel kissed Luxen's neck. Luxen blinked, unbalanced, unsure. Solomon had moved so fast Luxen hadn't even seen the blade in Solomon's hand, now pressed to his throat.

Solomon tilted his head and leaned in. All of his prettiness turned sharp and lethal, and those green eyes were no longer filled with wonder. "Don't think I won't kill you, demon."

The blade's steel edge dug in. From where he'd produced the blade, Luxen had no idea, but having his attack so elegantly thwarted and having Solomon almost close enough to kiss, but threaten him instead, might have been the most arousing thing he'd ever experienced. If there hadn't been a blade at his throat, he might have stolen a kiss just to see how it ruffled the angel's feathers. But this one *would* kill him.

Solomon stepped back and lowered his blade. "As we are to be chained together for several hours, I suggest you don't test me again." He turned with a sweep of his wings. Luxen smiled at the angel's leather clad back, and his overarching wings. He was beginning to understand why Mikhail and Konstantin held this one in such high regard. He wasn't all feathers. He had a bite too.

Solomon yanked on the chain, jerking Luxen along the overgrown pathway behind him.

"Where are we going?"

"You'll know when we arrive."

"We could fly." The chain wasn't so heavy that it would weigh them down. At least not for a short flight. Luxen so wanted to *fly*. He could smell the ocean, over London's odor of human traffic and the muddy river that snaked through its heart.

"It's not far."

Luxen wanted a great many things. To fly, to fuck, to feed. None of which it appeared he'd be getting anytime soon. Still, he was outside the enclosure, and that was one step closer to freedom. How difficult could it really be to outwit a single angel?

CHAPTER 4

olo

He'd known Luxen would try something. Truthfully, he'd have been disappointed if the ex-High Lord hadn't. Of course Solo wasn't going to chain a demon to himself without also having a means of defense should things get heated. A dagger-sized angelblade to the neck seemed to have deterred the ex-High Lord, for now. But Luxen would try again.

They wouldn't need to be chained together for long.

Firstly, he had to get Luxen out of the open. Somewhere safe, where they wouldn't be disturbed. Then he'd question him, secure the information he needed—as was their deal. He'd locate Samiel and return both demons to their enclosure, all by nightfall, when Severn was due to check in with an update on the missing key.

There was only one place Solo could take Luxen for

questioning where they wouldn't be disturbed. But as he approached the mid-terraced house with several cats sunning themselves on the steps outside, worry nibbled at his resolve. Somehow, in all of the madness, he'd adopted the human house as his home. Along with the cats, who perhaps had adopted him; he wasn't yet sure on that. Inviting Luxen inside would leave Solo vulnerable. Unless he pretended it was just another human house and not his personal sanctuary.

Besides, they were here now. He couldn't turn around without wasting more time.

Demons entering houses in this part of London wasn't as unusual as it would have been during the war, and nobody spared them a glance as Solo climbed the steps, shooing the cats aside.

"Vanish your wings," Solo suggested, with some force behind his tone.

Luxen ignored him and instead paused on the steps and glanced around them. He cut a distinctive silhouette with his sharp wings, naked chest, leather trousers, and knee-high buckled boots. If he were seen, there'd be no mistaking him for anyone besides the notorious ex-High lord.

Solo grabbed the demon by the arm and hauled him through the door, shoving him ahead with enough force to pinch his wings backward. Luxen growled and swore. A cat yowled from under his feet. He whirled in the narrow hallway, wings flicking out at awkward angles. One already stretched halfway up the stairs, the other pressed against the wall and ceiling. "Angel, touch me again and I'll rip the feathers from those pretty wings of yours." Light glinted off his sharp teeth and licked up his black horns.

Solo—his own wings already vanished—slammed the door. "Please, hide your wings while we're inside or we'll be stuck in this hallway."

Luxen's growl dissipated. He blinked and looked around the tiny hallway, only now realizing he was wedged. What had flustered him so? Surely not the demons outside? Perhaps it was the fact he'd been seen with an angel.

Finally the demon rolled his shoulders and his wings fizzled out of sight, banished from space, leaving a horned male no less imposing without his leathery wings to frame him. "Trust me, I don't want you here the same as you don't want to be here. But here we are." Solo's mood was souring by the minute. Time was not on their side, and if Severn caught him with Luxen outside the enclosure... well, the thought was too horrible to dwell on. It wouldn't come to that.

Solo pointed at the doorway into the front room. "Inside. Go."

"I see surrendering your sword has done nothing to temper your angelic holier-than-thou attitude."

"I didn't surrender it. I willingly plunged it into the earth as a sign of both defiance and strength. I'm not surprised you don't understand."

"So like a fucking angel." Luxen sneered and entered the front room. "What's with all the cats?"

Solo counted four inside the front room. Two on the couch, one on the windowsill, and one on a shelf. But not the missing one, Five. She was still absent. "Nothing. Sit down."

"I'll stand."

"Fine."

"Even now, you believe you're superior. You think you won the war, don't you."

"What I think doesn't matter. The war is over." Solo dropped the coiled chain with a loud metallic clatter. The cats sprang from their comfortable positions and bolted from the room in a scrabble of claws and blurred fur. He should feed them, but he had a much larger, more demanding pet to take care of.

"What?" Luxen frowned.

"Nothing."

"Why are you smiling?"

"Am I?" He tried to force the smile off his lips. "I was just thinking…" Luxen's face darkened. He wouldn't appreciate being called a pet. "Never mind. Let's get straight to it. You offered to help me find Samiel if I set you free, so here we are."

Luxen raised his shackled wrist. "This is not free."

"And I'm never letting you go. This is a compromise."

"No."

"But that was the deal."

"No, it wasn't." The demon folded his arms. "You changed the terms. So I'm changing them. If you won't let me go, then I need something else from you."

"What?"

"Feeding."

"Like a cat?"

Luxen blinked. "What?"

"Not that, then. I mean…" What did he mean? "I have some food in the kitchen—not that I'd know for certain, considering I clearly do not live here." This seemed to be going well. "Because this is not my house."

Luxen's frown had deepened. "I can't decide if you're deliberately irritating or if you're naturally like this?"

"Excuse me? Like what exactly?"

"Did you just compare me, a demon High Lord, to a cat?"

"Technically, Konstantin is High Lord."

"Mention that name again and we'll see how fast you can draw that blade from wherever you're hiding it."

"Konstantin's name?"

The air shimmered behind the demon, his wings threatening to reappear. Something fluttery and sharp danced in Solo's chest. He liked poking this demon, he realized. There was a thrill to it. Like when he teased the cats with string, knowing their claws could spring out at any moment. Only this cat was much bigger. Oh, but Solo wanted to see it.

Luxen dropped onto the couch cushions, leaned back, and folded his legs at the ankle, making himself at home. "I have time at my disposal. Time is all I have left. You, however, I suspect do not have much time. How long will it be until you're missed? Until an angel comes looking and finds you chained to me?" He rattled the chain on his arm, for emphasis. "Because I very much doubt you have approval to remove me from the enclosure." Luxen's smirk made the fine hairs on the back of Solo's neck stand erect. "I thought so."

Solo crossed his arms and huffed. He had known this wouldn't be straightforward. Nothing about Luxen was simple, but he may have underestimated the lord's willingness to be difficult. "I can make you sandwiches. What filling would you like?"

"Filling? Hm. I think you know, Solomon."

"I don't—" The sex. The innuendo came crashing open and the reason behind the demon's smirk struck him like a slap to the face. Of course the demon wanted the sex. Concubi fed from it. Any kind of emotion, really, as long as it was strong enough to summon ether, an aura most beings unknowingly exuded and concubi demons absorbed. Severn had absorbed Solo's ether while he had engaged sexually with a willing nephilim. "Oh."

"Your freckles darken when you blush."

His heart tried to leap from his chest. "Impossible."

"Not really, they darken in the same way your wings have a tendency to catch the light when you spread them—"

"Excuse me." He made it outside the room and halfway down the hallway before the chain snapped taut.

Solo stared at the chain, suddenly horrified he'd been the one to chain himself to this demon. What had he been thinking? He grasped the stair rods and bowed his head against them, like peering through bars. His lungs heaved, his body buzzing, thoughts whirring, blood pumping. His wings threatened to burst from their illusion. He fought to keep them hidden, but that was good, because it meant he wasn't thinking about Luxen, sprawled on the couch, a suspicious rod down the front of his leather pants.

Was he... aroused?

By Seraphim, what on earth had aroused him?

Luxen couldn't know how he'd thought about doing the sex with him. How he'd dreamed it, even? There had only been the nephilim Severn had paid for, and while that had been astonishing, amazing, like nothing he'd ever experienced in his entire life, it hadn't been the full sex, not how he'd researched since then. He knew how it worked. Even craved it. But it couldn't be with *Luxen*. Anyone else but *him*.

But he really, *really* needed to find Samiel. The light outside was fading. Time was passing him by. Severn would come soon.

He folded his right hand into a fist and squeezed his eyes closed. It didn't have to be the sex... Concubi fed on ether, and ether came from any strong emotion. What if he gave him a little bit? But how did one even do that? Luxen was a powerful concubi and Solo a novice when it came to such things. How could he stop Luxen from taking too much or going too far?

He couldn't do this. He just couldn't.

So why was his own member awake and filling? Why did it throb with want if he did not want Luxen?

He wished he did not feel this way. He wished he'd never kissed Mikhail on that rooftop and he wished Severn had never taken him to the nephilim.

Although, even all that was a lie. Because without these feelings, he'd be an empty shell, waiting to fall on his own blade so the world no longer hurt.

"Angel?"

Solomon groaned and hoped he didn't hear. *That voice*.

"As you seem to be struggling, I will also accept sandwiches in exchange for a fraction of the information I know."

Solo puffed out the breath he'd clung to. Yes. Sandwiches. Sandwiches he could definitely do.

CHAPTER 5

uxen

WHY LUXEN HAD GIVEN the angel an out with the sandwiches, he wasn't sure. Clearly Solomon found the idea of touching Luxen a repulsive one, so there was no point in extending both of their torture by demanding anything sexual, despite it being the easiest route to satisfying his hunger. There was the option of using allure on the angel, make him want sex and banish all his inhibitions, but that was tantamount to rape. And while Luxen had sometimes skirted the line of consent, he'd never crossed it. And he had no intention of doing so now, not even with an angel.

He'd have to endure the ache of want and eat sandwiches instead.

Solomon appeared in the doorway. "The chain won't reach into the kitchen..."

Luxen rose and followed the angel down the narrow hallway to the small kitchen at the rear of the house. His scent was everywhere, the house his, although he'd clumsily denied it. Luxen hadn't been aware angels lived in houses. He'd always believed they resided in grand chambers in Aerie. But this angel was different. He'd sensed that since meeting him. Different in subtle ways Luxen was still trying to fathom.

Leaning a hip against the kitchen countertop, Luxen watched Solomon open the fridge.

"I have salmon or tuna."

An angel was making him a sandwich in his own home. Would miracles never cease? "You choose." He'd brought sandwiches to Luxen's enclosure, but this was different—watching him bumble about the kitchen was more personal.

Solomon grabbed a bagged loaf of bread and a plate, and set to work making the sandwiches. "You could just tell me where Samiel is."

"I could."

Solomon had chosen tuna, and as soon as the tin was removed from the fridge, cats spilled into the kitchen. More cats than Luxen could count due to their whip-like speed through an open window and back door cat-flap. One decided to slink its silky black body against Luxen's boot and purr. He gave it a gentle shove.

Solomon noticed, scooped her up, and glared at Luxen.

He raised both hands. "I barely touched it."

Solomon popped the cat down on the countertop and muttered something then threw Luxen another accusing glare that almost had a laugh bursting free of him. He coughed into his hand instead and admired the kitchen, the cats, and the angel, making him a sandwich. This was all very... unexpected.

The black cat sauntered along the countertop and nudged Luxen's arm.

"*Two* is a terrible judge of character," Solomon said.

Luxen looked down to find the small cat peering up at him. *Two*. He gave Two a pat on the head, then frowned and pulled his hand back. What the fuck was he doing, making friends with an angel's cat? The cat purred and nudged him again. Luxen was supposed to be waiting for the angel to become distracted so he could knock him out, steal the key, and get free, not getting to know his pets.

Solomon cut the crusts off the sandwiches and with a harrumph, handed over the plate. "There. Now tell me where Samiel is so we can get this over with."

The plate was identical to the ones he'd been served in the enclosure. Had Solomon been making Luxen's sandwiches from his own kitchen this whole time? Luxen had assumed they'd come from Aerie, not Solomon's little kitchen, from his own supplies.

Solomon stepped back and leaned against the opposite counter. "What demon let Samiel out? Tell me that, at least. So we can move forward."

Luxen eyed the sandwiches, then the cats, who had all grouped around him, pointed ears erect and eyes shining. In truth, he didn't want to eat the sandwich, he wanted to eat *the angel*. On a whim, he knelt, set the plate down, and opened the sandwiches. The cats rushed him like sharks in a feeding frenzy.

"What game are you playing with me?" Solomon growled, which for him was a rumbling little throaty sound. "You want sandwiches, then you don't?"

"They look hungry."

"They are, but you—" The angel's face flushed. He turned his gaze away, but his cheek fluttered as he fought some unknown emotion. Luxen slid his focus out of clarity and caught sight of the angel's ether simmering off him in translucent waves. Not hate. *Fury*. He didn't want Luxen here, didn't want him in the house or near his furry pets, or even at the end of the chain. Solomon *despised* him.

That much fury, it had to have a reason behind it. "Did I do something to you, personally?"

"What?" His glare trained on Luxen.

"Have I hurt you or your kin?"

"Me?" Solomon laughed, but the sound was barbed. "No. And it's not the war, if that's what you're thinking. I know angels were ultimately the source of *everything*." His eyes narrowed. "You want to know why I'm angry at you, besides the obvious?"

"Yes." He wanted to know it so badly that if Solomon wanted to trade information on Samiel for it, he'd give it. It was important—part of the riddle that made up this unique angel. A riddle Luxen couldn't get enough of.

Solomon pushed forward and met Luxen eye to eye. He had to stand on his toes to do it. It put him so close that the angel's scent and ether swirled over Luxen, washing him in tantalizing ripples. This close, his creamy, freckled face was so porcelain-perfect that Luxen had to keep his hands locked at his sides to keep from reaching out and touching his jaw or tracing his soft pink lips. The fury made him all the more alluring.

"You took Mikhail," Solomon said with a sneer. "You took him, and you manipulated him, and you hurt him. It wasn't in battle, it wasn't the war. You did it because you could. And that... that is unforgiveable."

The angel's heated words had the strange effect of cutting into Luxen, making some long-forgotten fragile part of his heart hurt. "What's he to you?"

Solomon's lip turned up in a snarl. "It doesn't matter."

"You want to fuck him, is that it? And you think I got there first?" He wasn't sure why he'd said it. It was a petty comment, something a pup would say, and when Solomon's hand swung for Luxen's face, he let it happen. Wanted it, even. The crack, the burn; he gasped, absorbing the sudden rush of ether that rolled off Solomon, straight into him. Solomon snarled with tiny, blunt angel teeth. And the mental wall Luxen had built inside to hold back his own rage collapsed. His wings exploded outward. He grabbed Solomon's wrist, drove the angel back against the counter and slammed his mouth over his, thrusting his tongue in whether Solomon wanted it or not.

Ether rose in a tidal wave, mind-numbing, blinding, and blazing all at once. Fury, fear, but something else too... something Luxen knew well. Solomon writhed, his small body firm and trembling under Luxen's. Having Solomon against him flicked all Luxen's switches. The angel pushed, and a sharp snap of doubt doused Luxen's desire, only for it to surge back when Solomon's mouth opened and his sweet tongue swept in, definitely wanting. The taste of his ether went from bitter rage to smooth, sweet desire, and Luxen's whole body came alive for it, for *him*.

Yes, this was what he needed. This was what he was starved for. But more than just ether, he'd wanted his hands on this fiery angel since he'd first seen him.

Solomon pushed—his hands like brands on Luxen's

bare chest—and as Luxen eased back, Solomon danced Luxen across the small room, driving him against the opposite counter, so now Luxen was the one pinned under Solomon's weight. Angel wings shimmered into sight—a wall of red feathers rose and folded around them, like two shields of feathered fire.

Amidst the kiss, Luxen's breath caught. *Beautiful.*

It was the only word his addled brain could think up, especially when Solomon's left hand began to claw at Luxen's backside, and his right plunged between them to Luxen's crotch. Solomon was everywhere, his scent inside Luxen's head, his touch scorching his skin, his strength pinning Luxen down—he'd been right, Solomon's passion was an inferno waiting for someone to give it the oxygen to breathe.

Solomon tore from the kiss, leaving Luxen's lips tingling. He touched his own mouth. Shock widened his long-lashed eyes and his swollen lips parted in some silent cry. Luxen had no idea what was going on inside of the angel's head, but his heart ached to find out. He brushed his knuckles down Solomon's cheek, marveling at the angel's soft skin. A wonder to think something so beautiful could slay so many demons.

He should pull away. Solomon had to know it too, but he didn't move, and neither did Luxen. Want and desire and ether, confusion and pain, panic but also strength. He could read Solomon like a book. He was a mess, but he was also right on the verge of figuring something out.

He wanted Luxen. The desire in his ether was sweet rain on a summer day.

A knock sounded at the door.

Solomon sprang back and plastered himself against the

counter, wings spread, as though Luxen had thrown him there. "Oh no." He gripped the counter's edge. "No, no, no, no, no... This is bad. No."

Luxen almost went to him, told him to ignore the door so they could fuck—the angel wanted it, his body screamed for it, his ether throbbed with lust, and Luxen would happily let him climb his body and ride his cock all night long, which appeared to be the way that kiss had been going. But Luxen stayed back, sensing the angel was teetering on the edge of panic. He had no wish to shove him over the wrong side of it.

The knock sounded again. "Solo?"

Luxen knew that voice. *Konstantin*! Lust turned to ice in Luxen's veins. Konstantin, the traitor to all demonkin, was here! Luxen grabbed a knife from the nearby block. He had to make the traitor pay. He could end this fake peace if he ended Konstantin. He lunged for the door. Solomon dashed in front of him, blocking the hallway.

"Don't... Please don't," he whispered, wings spread, long red hair wild, like fire about him, all ruffled and spilled over his shoulders where Luxen might have grabbed at it. "Please, Luxen, no."

His name on Solomon's lips, the desperation on his face... Luxen's maddening rage spluttered and died.

"What's going on in there?" Konstantin growled. "Solo, open up or I'm coming in!"

Solo's face fell. "I'm coming!" he squeaked, but his face pleaded with Luxen. He extended his hand. "The knife... Hand it over."

He could cut down Solomon in a blink and attack Konstantin. It would probably be the last thing he did, probably get him killed, but it might be worth it.

"Please... don't do this. You don't want this."

But Solomon's face, the fear that threaded through his tangled ether, it wasn't just fear for Konstantin, he feared for Luxen too. And knowing that, Luxen couldn't hurt him.

"Solo! Open up, dammit!"

Luxen handed Solomon the knife. Not here, then. Another time. Another place. He wouldn't hurt this angel, it wouldn't be right.

Solomon backed up. His wings shimmered and vanished. "Don't," he said, reaffirming it, then turned his back on Luxen and headed for the front door.

CHAPTER 6

Solo

HIS HEART GALLOPED, trying to escape his chest. Panic almost had his wings bursting into sight all over again. His body burned from the kiss, and from... other things. And now Severn was here, on his doorstep, and Solo was still chained to Luxen. Severn would know. He'd know Luxen was here, and he'd burst in, and they'd fight, and one of them would die. That couldn't happen. He was protecting Severn, but also... strangely, Luxen.

Solo had to stop the pair from clashing, at any cost.

He stopped behind the door, took a deep breath, tried to wear an expression he hoped didn't look as though he'd had his hand on the ex-High Lord's thick member through his trousers, and definitely hadn't had his tongue tangling with the ex-High Lord's. His own member was so painfully hard he couldn't think around its insistent throb.

Oh by Seraphim, there was no way he could do this. But he had to. To stop them both from making a mistake.

He hid the knife behind his back, half opened the door, and peeked out.

Severn reeled, drew a breath, and shook his head, as though stunned. "Ugh... fuck... What the—" He pressed a hand to his forehead and took a few seconds to balance himself.

Solomon waited with the door hiding half his body, the half with the shackle on his wrist, the knife in his hand, and his erect member trapped inside his leather flight-trousers. Hopefully he appeared nonplussed and innocent, but given Severn's reaction, he suspected his ether had rendered all his efforts moot.

"Solo, fuck... Your ether—"

"Are you all right?"

"Am I all right?" Severn chuckled, lowering his hand and regaining his composure. "I've caught you at a bad time..." He tried to get a peek behind Solo, but Solo pinched the door against his body.

"I er... yes, I have some company."

"I can feel that." Severn's grin grew. "Who is he? Or she? Actually, no. Don't have to tell me. It's none of my business." He chuckled and stepped back down a few steps, giving him space. "You're good though, right?" He enquired. "You don't need any advice?"

"I think I have it, thank you." Oh gods, if his face grew any hotter he'd melt into a puddle.

"Dayam, I'd forgotten how hot you run. Anyway—" Clearing his throat, he continued. "I just dropped by to say the key *is* missing and there's no record of who took it, but as you're busy, you wanna carry on our discussion tonight?"

Anything, just so long as he left. "Er, yes, let's do that."

"How long do you need? An hour?" Severn smirked. "More? I'd leave you all night, but we do need to sort this *problem* as soon as possible."

"I'll er... An hour? Yes. I think an hour will be sufficient."

"All right, I'll meet you in Aerie then."

"Aerie...?" Had his voice pitched to new heights? He cleared it with a small cough.

"Is that a problem?"

"No. It's... I just..." *I have the ex-demon High Lord chained to me and he probably won't be welcome in Aerie.* But he couldn't say that so—"Okay."

"Great." Severn's eyebrows lifted. "Have fun, Solo." He took to the air, and soon as he was far enough away, Solo let out a relieved sigh and closed the door.

"Oh, by Seraphim..." He slumped against the wall and raised his chained hand to his forehead. Luxen loomed in the kitchen doorway, filling it with all of his innate demonness. Solo couldn't look at him. With his horns and wings out, he was too big to avoid.

Luxen had *kissed* him.

He'd forced Solo.

Maybe.

No. Maybe not.

It hadn't been like that.

Solo had wanted it... He'd wanted it so badly he'd almost jumped down the demon's throat. He'd pushed Luxen against the counter. He'd... *touched* him.

"Angel—"

Solo marched down the hallway, forcing Luxen backwards into the kitchen, and tossed the knife onto the countertop. Luxen opened his mouth, probably to say something smart and distracting and extremely sexy.

Solo pressed a finger to the demon's lips. "What just happened here, didn't. Do you understand? We didn't *do that*. We did not... It just—it didn't happen."

Luxen blinked, then his eyes narrowed, his gaze turning sly.

Wait, why wasn't Luxen fighting back, pushing him off? Why were his lips so soft? His smile so wicked. So enticing. Solo could take his finger and slide it between his lips and he knew without any doubt that Luxen would let him.

Solo jerked his finger back. What by Seraphim had gotten into him? This was *Luxen*. Severn's enemy. He was not to be toyed with. Even if it felt so good to play and touch...

"I'm sorry. I shouldn't have... done that," Solo muttered. He retreated across the narrow kitchen, which wasn't far enough away from the hole he'd found himself in but would have to do.

Luxen's brows pinched. "Sorry for what?"

He wasn't even sure. Everything was so messed up. So confusing. His body demanded one thing but his head wanted to shut all that down. There was only finding Samiel. Nothing else should even feature in his thoughts, and certainly not touching the demon who was supposed to be his prisoner. There was something wrong with him, wasn't there? Not for touching a demon, angels did that now, but because Luxen was *bad*. So bad. He even looked bad, with those low-slung leather pants and the way his hip was cocked to one side. By the gods, why was that thought making him want the demon *even more*. What was this madness?!

Luxen huffed, ruffled his wings and vanished them away, then propped himself against the counter again. "Calm down, angel, before your heart leaps from your chest."

"Calm down?" Solo breathed. Or tried to. His lungs had shrunk in his chest. *Calm down?* He'd kissed Luxen. And it hadn't been like when he'd kissed Mikhail *at all*. His kiss with Mikhail had been... mechanical. Good, but not the fireworks and electricity that kissing Luxen had ignited inside him. His lips still sort of tingled, and he could still taste Luxen's demony, herby taste, like rosemary... Gods! He was losing his mind.

"An angel freed Samiel," Luxen said, bringing Solo's spiraling thoughts to an abrupt halt.

Impossible. Solo snorted. "You expect me to believe that?"

"If you don't then why are we here?" Luxen rolled his eyes. "Why break me out if you're not going to listen?"

"I didn't break you out. This is just a temporary... excursion."

"Excursion?" One of the ex-High Lord's eyebrows shot up. "That Konstantin doesn't know about."

A growl rumbled through Solo. An angel couldn't have let Samiel go. That didn't make any sense. All angels knew Samiel was in cahoots with Luxen. "How do you know it was an angel?"

Luxen sighed. "Perhaps all the silvery feathers and the stick up his ass were a clue?"

Solo blinked. A strange little tickle began in his throat that almost wanted to be a laugh, but he definitely was not going to let it turn into one, so he swallowed it. "Demons can pretend to be angels," he said haughtily.

"A rare few. But none of us want to. Konstantin was the exception that proves the rule. It's extremely difficult to convincingly maintain an illusion like that for any length of time. Besides, I'd know an illusion, and that angel wasn't wearing one. He walked, talked, and smelled angel."

Solo screwed up his nose. He didn't want to know how angels smelled to demons. "So this angel walked into the enclosure, unlocked Samiel's door, and let him out? Just like that?"

"Exactly."

Why would Luxen lie? Hm, of course he would. He'd lie just to mess with Solo. But, as unlikely as it was, there was also the chance he was telling the truth, which meant an angel was actively sabotaging them. "Did he say anything, this *angel*?"

Luxen lifted a shoulder. "Nothing of merit."

"The angel and Samiel must have spoken?"

"He said something about Samiel being useful, and Samiel thanked him. That was it. They were rather in a hurry."

It didn't add up. An angel freed Samiel, but not an ex-High Lord? "And the angel didn't stop to talk to you? Didn't let you out?"

"Clearly."

Solo narrowed his eyes. Luxen didn't appear to be lying, but would Solo recognize his lies? "Why was that? He had a key. He could have freed you in seconds?"

"Perhaps he doesn't like me. When we find him, be sure to ask."

"Are you lying?"

Luxen's lips pinched. "Contrary to what you've probably been told, I don't lie with my every breath. Lying to you now serves no purpose. I could string you along with some tale about a dastardly demon. Would that better fit your narrative?"

Solo would not rise to that bait. "You'd know the angel again if you saw him?"

"Yes. His wings were distinctive."

Taking Luxen to Aerie to search for this angel was the next course of action, but how to ensure Mikhail didn't find out? Perhaps now was the time to tell Mikhail about all of this? If an angel was involved, Mikhail had a right to know. But there was the European Guardian's visit, and Severn had made it clear Mikhail was not to be involved. Not yet. And Luxen probably wouldn't want to be paraded around Aerie. It was bad enough he'd been chained to Solo.

This whole thing was turning out to be a disaster. Samiel escaping, an angel being the one to let him out, kissing Luxen...

No, not thinking about that.

But there was a place in Aerie Solo knew, a secret place, where he could take Luxen to observe the angels without anyone knowing.

"All right, after sunset, we'll fly to Aerie."

"You want *me* to go to Aerie?" His smirk faded.

"It's not... It's different now. You'll see."

"I really don't care to see your palace of monsters."

"You said you wanted to fly."

The big demon's eyes narrowed and all his sly humor fell away. "You say such things as though they're trivial. I've observed Aerie from below for much of my long life. I grew up knowing it as a hive of demon-killers." Luxen lifted his chained wrist. "And you're taking me there in chains. It hasn't changed, angel. It's the same pretty nest of killers it's always been."

Solo shifted, uncomfortable. He'd forgotten they'd been mortal enemies, but Luxen's opinion of Aerie had brought it all back. "For what it's worth, I'm sorry... for all of it."

"It's not for you to be sorry."

He didn't know what else to say to fix Luxen's rapidly declining mood. Or the past between them. Words weren't enough to mend those old wounds.

They had an hour to wait until sundown. "So we'll just wait, I guess." He sounded confident, but didn't feel it. Tension sizzled in the air, as though striking a match might set the whole house ablaze. And as the minutes ticked over, that strange sizzling heated Solo's skin.

He busied himself cleaning up the sandwiches the cats had licked clean and then poured glasses of water for himself and Luxen. Luxen drank his down without stopping for breath, making his throat undulate in a way Solo had to tear his gaze from. They'd both vanished their wings so they didn't crowd the kitchen, but the air still felt cramped and suffocating.

Twenty minutes after Severn had left, the tension had become so much that if Solo chewed on his lip any more, he'd bite clean through it. He had to get outside before whatever this was boiled over and he did something stupid like kiss Luxen again.

"Angel," Luxen said. He was leaning on the kitchen countertop and peering outside through a window. Shirtless, his bare back proved an impossible temptation to avoid admiring.

"My name is Solomon," Solo grumbled. He rinsed out the glasses.

"Konstantin called you Solo."

"Yes, but he and I are friends. And you and I are not."

"We aren't?" Luxen purred.

"No." They were still enemies. A kiss didn't change that. Did it?

"Then what are we?"

He was teasing, but Solo wasn't rising to that bait. "Enemies."

"Enemies who tongue-fuck."

Tongue-fuck. Solo nearly choked on his. "We're not talking about *that*."

"Oh yes. I forgot. And are we also denying how hard your precious angel cock was when you rubbed it against me? Just so we're clear on the details, should anyone ask."

Hs member had been no such thing. And he couldn't stand another second trapped inside the tiny house with Luxen pressing his buttons.

He gathered up the chain and pulled the demon into motion behind him, glancing back to make sure Luxen ducked through the doorway without bashing his horns. Luxen was smirking again, and doing that thing where he walked as though every step was designed to lure Solo in, as though he might pounce at any second.

He'd had his hand firmly planted on Luxen's warm ass and recalled how he'd ground the demon against him and felt... his arousal rub against his own. Even with their leather garments between them, he'd still felt the slow grind.

Already at half-mast, Solo's member began to tingle and fill. No, no, no... He needed to get out of the house and his mind off the sex. He flung open the front door and dashed down the steps, hauling Luxen behind him. "All right, we're going to fly—"

Luxen's wings burst open with a loud crack and the demon took off like a rocket. Solo dropped the chain to keep it from getting tangled around his arms, then thrust his own wings open and pushed into the air to avoid being dragged there by Luxen and the chain.

Luxen's leathery wings flapped, sounding like sheets in the wind. Solo's whispered with every push. But despite the mechanical way Luxen's wings worked to lift him higher, there was a beauty to each stroke that angel wings didn't have. Every muscle was displayed, nothing hidden. The wing membrane stretched, thinning, making the veins light up like forks of lightning in a night sky. Solo found himself almost envious of the demon's no-nonsense flight. Of course, his own was effortless, each of his red feathers providing lift, but a demon in flight was a symphony of muscle and movement all of its own.

The air had a damp twang to it, the taste of London. Above the clouds, the air would be thinner and cleaner, but Luxen wasn't climbing higher. He made for East London, toward demon territory. Solo allowed it, if only because he was enjoying the view from behind. Occasionally, Luxen glanced over his shoulder and wing to check Solo was close. He had to be, the chain kept him close, but he looked anyway. And after the third or fourth glance, Luxen's smile grew. Not a smirk, not even a salacious grin, just an honest smile. Solo thought it might have been the first time he'd seen the demon lord's true smile.

Luxen tucked his wings in and spiraled down. The chain spiraled too, spinning, leaving Solo with no choice but to clamp his wings together and dive while corkscrewing to keep the chain from knotting in the air. If it tangled too much, it would pull them into each other.

Luxen either didn't care about the risk or he wanted Solo to get tangled in the chain. Hm... Perhaps that was the demon's plan. An uncontrolled fall from this height would kill an angel.

Luxen rocketed skyward.

The chain snapped taut.

Solo flung his wings out in an effort to slow himself so the chain didn't rip his arm off, but it still yanked him out of his flightpath and whipped him around like a fly on the end of a fishing line. He flailed, wings flapping to catch him upright, but the sky spun. He couldn't find the horizon, couldn't find the *up*. He grasped at air.

A dark blur flew in, slammed into Solo, and scooped him out of his chaotic tumble.

Luxen laughed a deep rumbling, honest laughter. "You're like a fledgling falling from the nest."

How dare he! Solo levered him away enough to get a knee between them and kicked. Luxen flew backward. The chain lifted, rising between them, and Solo cartwheeled in the air, coming back down in control. He caught the chain and snapped it tight. Luxen's wings buckled. The demon lost his balance and tumbled, wings flapping madly behind him. "Not so smooth now!" Solo called after him.

Solo grinned, then dove, flung open his wings in great arches beneath Luxen, and caught the demon in his arms. The shocked expression on Luxen's face made it all worth it. "I warned you not to test me."

"Oh, I've just begun." Luxen bucked from his arms, flapped his wings so close that their claw-tipped arches almost cut his cheek, and then he was rising again, taking the chain with him. Solo caught its length and pulled, determined to control whatever was happening, but even his pumping wings couldn't hold the chain and the demon when he spiraled downward. Solo flapped with everything he had, but he was losing height to Luxen—dragged irrevocably downward by gravity and Luxen's spinning. The demon had perfect control of himself in the air—of course he did. Just because they didn't have feathers didn't make them any less capable in flight. In fact, Solo knew demons to be more maneuverable than angels, often having the advantage in battle during stormy weather.

Solo flapped, heaved, flapped again, and looked down to see Luxen climbing the chain, something wicked and gleeful on his face that set Solo's heart racing for different reasons.

Luxen almost made it. Solo dropped the last length and arched head over heels, looping around and underneath Luxen. The demon gave a squawking laugh, then growled and lunged. Laughter bubbled out of Solo too. He dove, spotted a few high-rises above, and launched toward them.

He zipped and darted between them, Luxen close behind. *Gaining*. Making Solo's heart race.

Wait. What was this? Were they... playing?

Solo's laughter died.

Was this... He clenched a hand over his heart. What was this feeling?

Luxen struck, plucking Solo out of the air. Huge wings carried Solo higher, and even though they were a mile high, even though his enemy had caught him, it felt... *good*. He lifted his gaze, saw Luxen's smile. On meeting Solo's stare, the demon's dark eyes suddenly widened. Something bright and sharp struck at Solo's heart. He gasped, breathless.

An angel shot out from nearby cloud cover—just passing through—but his sudden appearance startled Luxen. He let Solo go.

Solo flung out his wings to keep from falling, but the motion of Luxen's snapped the chain tight again, jerking them both off-balance. The chain spun, tangling in itself, growing heavy and cumbersome, like a wrecking ball swinging dangerously between them. Luxen flapped unevenly. Solo desperately tried to hold it, but the lopsided swing tugged him down, and then the chain unlooped, freeing itself, but yanking on Luxen. The demon tilted, the chain pulled, and *down* he spiraled, tangled in the links.

Solo heaved, trying to keep both chain and demon in the air, but the chain yanked, and now they both tangled together. "Oh no." He swooped, diving in front of Luxen, and flung open his wings beneath them. Demon and chain slammed into his back. He barked a cry. Luxen fell off one side, the chain slid off the other, and now Solo was tangled in their mass, caught between them. The world spun again, but only long enough for him to realize they were falling too fast. He slammed into a flat roof with a heavy, bone-jarring thump. Luxen slammed into it a second later and the chain rained over them both.

"Angel?" Luxen croaked. "Solomon!"

Solo rolled onto his back and flicked out his wings, freeing them from underneath him, then peered through his hair at Luxen's fraught face.

"Idiot. What were you thinking?" Luxen snarled.

"Me?" Solo blinked at the darkening night sky. "You're

the one who took off like a wild thing." He coughed. Nothing felt broken. Bruised, stunned, but not broken.

Luxen shoved at the chain, untangling himself, then kicked it off. "You could have been killed," the demon grumbled, shaking the chain from his boot.

"You say it as though you didn't plan for exactly that to happen." That surely must have been his reason for all of the aerobatics. Why else would he dance with an angel?

Luxen got to his feet and brushed his scuffed leather trousers down. His chest was scuffed too, scratched and bleeding in places. A pang of guilt squeezed Solo's heart. He ignored it. The demon had just tried to kill him and he felt sorry for him? He really did have to get these emotions in check.

Luxen offered his hand and when Solo glared at it, he said, "Don't we have to visit Aerie to find your saboteur?"

Solo eyed the demon's hand with its sharp claw-like nails. Still breathless, still strangely tingly all over, he reached up and took Luxen's hand. There was no sudden snap of emotion, no dart of lust. Had he expected there to be? The demon helped haul him to his feet and stepped back as Solo shook grit off his feathers and gave them some hefty experimental flaps to ensure nothing was broken.

When he looked back at Luxen, the demon was blank-faced and impassive, but he'd clenched his hands into fists. Was he angry he'd failed in killing Solo?

"I am not so easy to kill." Solo coughed again and cleared his throat. He scooped up the chain. "Can you fly?"

"I'm fine." Luxen's wings twitched behind him. "Let's get this over with."

Bruised, and feeling the strain from a testing day, Solo

lifted off, into the cool dusk air. He checked Luxen was fine and could fly without wheezing or wobbling, earned a stare full of hatred, and climbed higher, heading for Aerie at a more sedate pace than their earlier aerobatics. The sooner they found the angel who had helped Samiel, the sooner Solo could put Luxen back into the enclosure. Even if the thought of doing so filled him with dread.

CHAPTER 7

Luxen

SOMETHING WAS WRONG, and it wasn't just the bruised wing he'd earned after slamming into the rooftop. When he'd pulled Solomon into his arms mid-flight, he'd felt mental armor crack and fall away, as though a part of him had been exposed, a vulnerable part revealed because of an angel.

Which was impossible.

And then there was the fact Solomon could have been killed when they'd gotten tangled in the chain.

He should want him dead.

He *did* want that.

Solomon was his ticket to freedom.

Yet...

Luxen had to get this over with. The longer he spent around the red-haired angel, the more the feathered fiend got under his skin and made him *care*. Did angels have their own allure? Because Solomon had to be working some kind of power over Luxen for him to *fear* the angel's death instead of wishing for it.

They flew high, to where the air was clear and thin and the stars shone. Aerie shimmered like a collection of suspended moonlight pools with a murky London below. Solomon took an indirect flightpath high above Aerie, and then swooped down at the last moment to land on an extended balcony. Luxen hovered, ignoring the fiery pain in his fractured wing, and waited for the angel to open the balcony's double doors and step inside. After he landed, he pushed through a thin gauze of curtain into a large bedchamber. Soft lights blinked on, illuminating an antiseptic space. The enormous double bed was neat, its cotton sheets perfectly tucked in. Pillows were fluffed. And then in another area, a knee-high glass table surrounded by large purple and pink cushions seemed to indicate an area for relaxing. It was all so very... pristine. The kind of look humans tried to emulate with their pastel colors and fluffy cushions. Luxen much preferred cool, dark silk, leather, and mahogany. Not cotton and feathers.

"Let me see your wing," Solo said, his face severe. All the laughter from their earlier flying games had vanished from his eyes. A laughter Luxen had been so surprised to see that, for a few moments, he'd forgotten they were enemies. He'd... enjoyed being with Solomon.

"There's no time for that," he snapped. "Why are we here?"

"You're hurt."

"What is this place?"

"This is—was my chamber. I don't use it much now."

An angel's bedchamber. Luxen had never thought he'd see one. He'd heard of how they lived in sparkling cages high in the clouds, so unlike demons down on the streets. Demons joked as to whether angels even had beds, or if they preferred to perch on branches.

Luxen drifted deeper into the room. "Why not? You don't like it?"

"Aerie..." He sighed. "It was never a home, not really."

No, Luxen could see that. The angel who stood in the middle of the chamber now no longer fit the space. He wore demon leathers, so dark against such pristine edges. His hair was a tousled mess, although that could have been the trials of the day. He'd worn it braided in tails whenever he'd guarded the enclosures. He didn't wear his angelblade, but with his arms crossed and his chin up, he looked as though he should. The angel he'd been in this place wasn't the same angel he was now. This one was more complicated, more layered in ways Luxen secretly wanted to pick at and expose.

Under Luxen's scrutiny, Solomon lowered his chin and looked away. "I witnessed my own kind turn on Mikhail. I was there, saw them do nothing when Remiel pushed him over the edge. If it hadn't been for Severn..."

The fact Konstantin had saved Mikhail was another reason the new High Lord betrayed his own kind.

"They did the same to you, no?" Luxen had his spies. He'd heard how Solomon should have died and was instead saved by the same demon who had appeared during the final battle. The same demon rumored to be the demon god, Aerius. He wasn't sure what he believed. Demons liked to talk. But there was no denying Mikhail had sported Seraphim's six wings and he had summoned the power of the gods. So was it too far a stretch to believe Aerius had been among them too? Yet, it seemed absurd that the demon god would save an angel.

"Your wing?" Solomon started forward, ignoring Luxen's question.

Luxen backed up. "I said it's fine."

Solomon frowned, but hung back. "All right."

"Why *did* Aerius save you?"

The angel blinked his soft lashes. "Because, I think, they blamed themself for losing Seraphim. They'd been trying to make it right ever since."

Luxen huffed a laugh and crossed the final few steps between them, making Solomon look up to face him. "Do you believe that fairytale? That a demon fell in love with an angel?"

Solomon stared back, his face contemplative. "I've seen it."

Luxen snorted. "In Konstantin and Mikhail? Please don't waste your breath… Do you know what I see? A mass-murderer fucking the king of the people he tried to wipe out. Mikhail hasn't changed. His ego loves all this. None of you angels are capable of change. When you don't get your way, you'll revert back to killing. It's in your blood."

"No, you're wrong. We were lied to. We *are* changing."

"I've yet to see proof. Just because you stuck your swords in the ground we're supposed to trust you now?" Luxen couldn't resist any longer and touched Solomon's smooth cheek. "Never going to happen, Solo."

Solomon's hand caught his wrist. "Do you think I'm the same? I haven't changed?"

Luxen lifted his other wrist, the one locked inside a shackle. "Prove you have. Free me."

He released the wrist he could free. "You know I can't do that."

"Because it would require you trusting me? Like I'm supposed to trust you now?" He laughed. "So very angel." He turned away before Solomon saw too much on his face. They were all the same. All killers underneath all the fine words and preened feathers.

"What happened to you?" Solomon asked in a soft, quiet voice. "Not the war. It wasn't that. Something else... Someone hurt you."

"Every demon has been hurt." Luxen pushed the curtain aside and stepped out onto the balcony. Among the stars, angels and demons silhouettes danced. Luxen snarled at them and stepped to the very edge of the balcony. No rail. Just a long drop to London far below. The wind swirled around him, stroking his wings, urging him to fly. He would, if he wasn't chained to an angel. Although he wasn't sure what he had to fly back to. The demons had made their choice in High Lord Konstantin. Luxen was nothing. No manor, no territory. His whole life had been climbing the ranks to reach the position of High Lord, only to have Konstantin rip it away.

He sensed Solomon behind him but hadn't heard him approach. Angels were stealthy like that, with their soft feathers and light feet. Terrors in the night. "When I was a pup, long ago," Luxen said, "I was afraid of stars." Solomon was silent for so long that Luxen had to glance behind him to check he was there.

The angel stood in shadow, his arms crossed, his wings relaxed behind him. "I don't know what to say."

"No, I imagine you don't." He smiled ironically. "Before I understood how the world worked, every star was an armored angel about to swoop down and take everything. Because that was what you did. So on clear nights like this, I hid. And learned to hate."

"We took your kin from you?"

Luxen watched the angels and demons dance again and ignored the strange tightness in his chest. "I don't remember much of it. Just that I was too small to fight them. I've been alone ever since."

"But... you were High Lord. You had... a harem?"

Luxen laughed at that. "You can appear to have everything and still be alone. I think you perhaps know what that feels like?"

The angel lowered his gaze and whispered, "I'm sorry."

"Sorry. Hm. A pathetic word. It changes nothing." Luxen faced the dark skies again. If he looked back, he'd see pity on the angel's face. "Did Konstantin tell you I'm not to be trusted? Did he tell you I'd manipulate you? There's a reason for that. Demon hierarchy is based on strength and virility. I'm not and never have been the strongest—if the world were fair I'd have been killed as a pup. But I learned to be clever. I learned to maneuver others so I didn't have to fight them to climb to the top. All I had to do was outsmart them. I had others fight my battles for me."

"Like how you had Samiel manipulate Severn?" Solomon stopped beside him at the edge of the balcony. His feathered wings brushed Luxen's, but he didn't twitch them away, and Luxen rather liked the soft whisper of feathers against his wing's leathery membrane.

"Severn—Konstantin turned against his own kind. I was protecting my people from the threat he'd become."

"And how you planned to manipulate Mikhail?"

"I underestimated Mikhail. And paid for it." He raised his shackled wrist. "You want to believe I'm bad, I'm the wicked demon who deserves to be punished? I understand. But I am the product of a war I couldn't win. I fought my own kind to survive, and then led the lords in battle against angels. I won't apologize for that. You blame me for hurting your precious Mikhail, when it was angels who put me on this path all those years ago, under those stars."

"Why are you telling me this?"

"Because you're the first angel to listen."

"For what it's worth, angelkind failed a great many people. Our own and yours. Change starts with recognizing our failures and wanting to make it right. We do want to change."

"Such pretty words." Luxen smirked. "From a pretty angel."

Solomon's mouth ticked up at one corner. "Come. We have an angel and a demon to find." He stepped off the edge in a blast of feathers, forcing Luxen to leap after him to keep the chain from yanking him into the air. His wing barked in pain, but he endured it and followed the angel's flight higher.

If more angels were like this one, Luxen could almost be persuaded they were capable of change.

If more angels were like this one, peace between races might actually stick.

CHAPTER 8

Solo

Focusing on finding Samiel kept his mind off how Luxen was proving to be more intriguing than he could have ever imagined. To know he'd been afraid of stars because he'd thought them angels... His whole life had been one long fight for survival. It hurt to think of other demon pups like him, their fear turning to hate. Hurt to think of Luxen being alone.

That cycle had to end.

He flew high, then tucked his wings together and dove downward, darting between the crevices where Aerie's domes met. A few zips left and right, and he flung out his wings, slowing to a sudden stop that almost had Luxen plowing into him. The demon grumbled and Solo hid his own smirk as he landed on the transparent glass roof. He knelt and waited for Luxen to do the same, then brushed dust from the glass, revealing Aerie's central chamber below and countless angels and demons passing through it.

Luxen's eyes widened. "They can't see us?"

"No. The lights inside prevent them from seeing this exact spot."

"You continue to surprise me. You like to spy on your own kind, angel?"

"No! That's not..." The demon smirked again. Solo ruffled his feathers. "If you must know, I came here after each battle and watched them to remind me what I fought for."

"Then this is your private hidey hole in the sky."

Was he secretly laughing? Solo narrowed his eyes.

"It's all right, I won't tell anyone."

He *was* laughing inside.

"I still have my blade, you know."

The demon's gaze trawled over him, setting Solo's skin ablaze and making his every feather tingle. "I'm intrigued to know where."

Did everything have to be innuendo with concubi? Or was that just Luxen? "Lie down."

"What?"

"Get down on your front. It's worth it. Trust me."

Luxen frowned at the dusty glass.

With a chuckle, Solo brushed more dust aside. Lifting his wings back, he laid himself on the glass, facing down. Luxen still frowned, but at the rise of Solo's eyebrows, he relented and crawled forward on his front, then laid down, wings stretched back.

"Okay," Luxen said, somewhat warily.

"Now you're floating over Aerie without flying."

Solo watched him fold his wings together and tuck

them against his back. He seemed to relax a little and, folding his arms in front of him, he peered through the glass. "All right. It's a good view."

It felt like a victory and Solo smiled at the demon sprawled on his front. He also took a moment to admire Luxen's body. Dark hair flowed around his horns, curiously glossy and soft, for their ordeal of the past few hours. The veins in his wings beat gently to the rhythm of his heart. If Solo touched those wings, they'd be warm, even in the cold night air. Luxen's bare lower back had neat little dimples. The rise of his ass, clad in leather pants, had Solo's flighty heart racing. Strong thighs, but lean. Long legs, wrapped in boots. When his wings were open, they were among the most impressive Solo had ever seen, besides Severn's.

"I know you're staring. You'd best stop. Or you will not like the consequences."

He should stop. They had an angel to find. By now, Konstantin would be searching for Solo. He needed a lead to alleviate some of the High Lord's rage when he learned how Luxen was out of the enclosure. But Solo *really* wanted to touch those wings.

"So many feathers..." Luxen muttered, watching the angels below. "Too many demons. Have they all forgotten what our kin died for?"

In his imagination, after he'd touched those wings, he'd stroke Luxen's naked back and over the rise of his ass. He knew when males mated, they could... enter there... and that it was pleasurable in a different way to having his member caressed, but he wasn't sure how, or why. He'd tried to use a human phone device to search on their internet for videos, but the screen had been so full of swollen members and wet holes and moaning that, by

Seraphim, he hadn't known where to look and had thrown the phone in the Thames—much to the human's dismay. He'd paid tokens, bought them a new one, and vowed never to search the internet for the sex again.

"Hm... he looks promising," Luxen said, focused on the task at hand. "No, never mind. Different wings. The one who freed Samiel had silvery wings, fading to dark tips. Feathers like polished steel."

Luxen's wings parted, opening some as he relaxed, and their folded arches came within reach. Just a little stroke... Would he mind? Surely not. Solo extended his hand, fingers twitching. Just a little touch... His fingertips touched the wing's edge, just the smallest of brushes. Luxen didn't react, so Solo trailed his touch lower. So warm. And not as rough as he'd expected. Like supple leather warmed in the sun. Lovely. Luxen's wing shifted outward, an inch closer to Solo, freeing more space to explore. Solo dipped his touch off the boney arch and down, over the folded membrane with its warm ripples. Touching Luxen was a treat, a wonder he never thought he'd experience. Sadly, Solo had grabbed enough demon wings during battle to know their feel, but this was different.

He skipped his fingers off the wing and, without thinking, ran his fingers down Luxen's bare back, sweeping over where the dimple pooled, and then up the smooth curve of his ass.

Luxen still hadn't moved, although he must have felt everything. As he gave no protest, Solo danced his fingers across Luxen's lower back. There, he did move. He shifted, just a fraction, and the muscles of his back adjusted in synchronicity with those of his shoulders, holding his wings up. His wings lifted higher, opening above and creating a canopy, and Solo hooked a leg over Luxen's, then rose to straddle the demon from behind. He couldn't think; thinking was bad—doing was good. He wanted both hands on the demon's back, and now he had them there, massaging up his muscular sides and then skimming down his spine. When Solo's hands reached the midpoint between Luxen's wings, he shivered but he made no noise of protest, no sound to stop Solo.

Was this right?

Was it *good?*

Solo bit his lip and stroked Luxen's back, kneading muscle in places and stroking in others. It felt good. His own wings had spread behind him. He kept them tucked under Luxen's so they didn't clash.

Solo's body throbbed. His member was rock-hard and aching with need. Did Luxen know how touching him made Solo want things? He had to. Concubi could smell lust, could taste it in his ether. And Solo was basking in it.

Was this how Mikhail and Konstantin did... the sex? Would Luxen even want that with him? Solo lowered his hands to the demon's leather-wrapped ass, cupped his buttocks, and dug his fingers in.

The moan that peeled from Luxen sounded wrought with pain.

Solo jolted his hands away. "I'm sorry! I don't... I don't know. I didn't mean..." He clambered off Luxen's legs and scooted back. What had he been thinking? He'd had his hands *all over him!* He looked at his hands—the traitors. And his member pounded inside his trousers—stretching the leather. Luxen would see!

Luxen was growling now, each breath like boulders

rolling together. He flicked his wings, rose onto his hands and knees, and turned around. His eyes blazed, and sharp teeth glinted behind sneering lips.

Oh Seraphim... Solo had done something terrible. Except, when Solo's gaze skipped down the demon's chest, past erect nipples and down, the male's impressive member had almost burst from his pants. Oh, he was hard. Was that good? That meant he was aroused, not... angry? Or maybe both at the same time?

This was so confusing.

"I think... we should... focus on..."

Luxen pounced, knocking Solo flat on his back, his wings pinned. His hot mouth scorched Solo's, tongue driving in, seeking, and Solo returned the kiss, driving himself deeper. Sharp teeth nicked his lip, and he didn't care. He grabbed at Luxen's shoulder, at his back, holding him close. Luxen's chained arm dropped. His hand rode down Solo's leathers with force enough he could feel its weight, and then it was there, over Solo's hungry member, squeezing.

Oh gods, what madness was this?

Solo's back arched, his body bucking without any notion of control. He wanted *more*. More of everything. More of Luxen's hand grinding him, more of Luxen's tongue fighting him, more of Luxen *everywhere*. His spiciness, his heat, his strength and weight.

His hand rubbed Solo's member. His growls rumbled. He broke from the kiss and stared deep into Solo's eyes. Solo moaned, gritted his teeth, and stared back, *demanding* more.

Luxen tore at Solo's pant ties, nails scratching, fingers yanking, and then all at once Solo's veined member was free and in the demon's hand. He loosed a cry, almost a whimper, from relief. *Yes, yes!* Thick fingers pumped. Luxen's eyes glowed, swimming with ether. "Yes, angel, I'm going to make you come for me."

Yes. Gods, yes. Tiny fireworks danced down Solo's spine, gathering low down, pressure building. He clutched at Luxen's shoulder, watched his wings flex, watched his lips tip into a wicked grin. "Come for me, come hard." Luxen slammed a kiss into Solo, and his pumping quickened. All reason and control abandoned Solo, until he was just a creature made of cresting pleasure, with no way out but to—

The pressure broke, his body spasmed, and he tore from Luxen's kiss and cried out, his member so full of heated pulsing, it was almost painful. Ripples barreled through him, wringing the last drops free.

He came down from the high on his back, wings pinned a little awkwardly, with Luxen sprawled over him, his eyes hooded and pupils blown. Oh dear... This was...

He had completely lost his mind.

There was no other explanation.

Luxen swooped in, his mouth hovered over Solo's, his eyes filling Solo's vision. "There is no shame in this, angel. Don't let their lies take pleasure from you."

He had been about to panic. Fear and shame and regret—it had all been waiting in the wings to rush in and drown him, but the way Luxen gazed at him now, and how his words built walls to hold all those negative feeling back... It worked. He wasn't ashamed. A demon had hold of his tingling cock, and he wasn't disgusted. There was nothing wrong in this. How could there be, when it felt so right?

He reached up and hooked a length of Luxen's dark hair behind his right horn.

Luxen's smile softened all of him. He tucked Solo's member back inside his trousers and deftly retied them. When he withdrew, Solo feared looking down at himself to find the mess of spend that was surely waiting, but much of it had been swept away. Luxen had cleaned him up.

The demon knelt on a knee and offered his hand. He seemed to sense Solo's hesitancy and said, "It's all right."

Was it? Really?

He took Luxen's hand and when the demon pulled, Solo didn't resist, and now he was tucked against Luxen's chest where he could hear his steady heartbeat. A sound so lovely, Solo could almost doze there.

"You know, I told myself when the blast of familiar ether hit, that everything was fine... but I'd check, just in case."

Severn.

Solo sprang from Luxen's arms and darted in front of him. Blocking Severn, but he couldn't block the sound of Luxen's growl. Severn had landed several feet away, wings half-spread, thick arms crossed, and with a glower that would have once dropped Solo to a knee.

Solo held out his hand, chain rattling. "Stop. It's not what you think."

"Your strange behavior? The lies? And now this... It's all very clear. *Luxen*."

"Konstantin." Luxen was on his feet, wings open, hands at his sides.

"What was your plan? Manipulate Solo to get him here, to us... Close to Mikhail so you could take a second shot at seducing him?" Severn reached behind his shoulder and withdrew an angelblade.

"No! Stop!" Solo staggered forward. "Stop, that's not what's going on."

"Get out of the way, Solo," Severn warned.

Luxen snarled. "Always the same, Konstantin. Reach for a blade instead of words. How very angel of you." He stepped forward.

Solo pushed at Luxen's chest. "Stop, both of you!"

"There is no way Solo would *touch* a snake like you." Severn's grip flexed on the huge two-handed sword. "I should have killed you long before now." With a roar, he charged.

CHAPTER 9

Solo

THE WORST CASE scenario was happening and Solo had a split second to act—*to choose*. Severn or Luxen? He didn't *know*! Luxen wasn't anything like he'd been told, but what did Solo really know of the ex-High Lord? Could Solo have been tricked into this, manipulated to bring Luxen to Aerie? That didn't seem right at all, but Severn *knew* Luxen. Had been raised with the lord. Solo had known him for a few weeks, and much of that had been with glass between them.

Severn had to be right, so why then did this feel so wrong?

Solo plunged in front of Severn and threw his wings open, shielding Luxen behind him. "Stop, Severn!"

Even then, the look of pure murder in Severn's eyes

reminded Solo exactly how demons could kill as readily as angels.

Severn snarled and tried to maneuver around Solo. Solo danced one way, then the other, blocking Severn's every step. "No! Stop this, *Konstantin*. Stop." He deliberately used Severn's demon name as a reminder of who he'd been before. It worked.

Severn growled and backed up, lowering the blade. "He has you under his allure. I can smell it on you, Solo. I should have known. I should have been more vigilant. You should never have been charged with guarding him."

Luxen chuckled. "Look at you, the demon High Lord, pulled up short by a single lowly angel."

Solo glared over his shoulder at Luxen and the demon smirked back. "Is it true?" Solo asked. "Did you lie to get me to bring you here?"

Luxen arched an eyebrow. "You have to ask?"

"Your allure? Did you somehow *make* this happen? Did you take my choice from me?!"

Luxen's eyes widened, then narrowed. "What if I did? I've been locked in that prison for weeks, shut away, starved, treated like an animal—worse than an animal. He was killing me through indecision!" Luxen stepped toward Severn. "At least have the balls to strike me down by your own hand, you traitorous coward."

Solo slammed a hand into Luxen's chest. He dared not look back at Severn. He'd barely been able to stop him from killing Luxen, something Luxen seemed too determined to have happen.

Luxen's gaze flicked to Solo's face. His rage fell away and his eyebrows pinched together.

Don't do this, Solo begged silently. Luxen's snarl faded. He *was* listening. Solo could stop him, but not Severn. He had to get them apart.

"I will take him back to the enclosure," Solo said, still eyeing Luxen, keeping him fixed to the spot.

"No." Mikhail landed so lightly nearby it was as though he'd been there all along. He folded his enormous black wings behind him. "I will."

Solo swallowed. Oh no... They were all in dire trouble now. He almost dropped to his knee but caught himself at the last second.

Luxen snorted a laugh. "Cowards, all of you." He snarled at Konstantin. "Locking me up. Isolating me? This is *not* the demon way, and you know it. You want me dead, then see it done."

Severn's eyes flared. "Come at me again and I will end it as demons do."

Luxen would. He tensed to do exactly that.

"No!" Solo snapped at them both. "He is a witness in... Samiel's disappearance." He couldn't meet Mikhail's gaze. Shame crawled over him. One mistake after another. He'd failed at every step. He didn't even deserve to be in Aerie. He unlocked the shackle, carried it and the key to Mikhail, and knelt. "Your Grace, please escort Luxen back to the enclosure. Samiel is missing. Luxen was helping me. I will explain everything on your return."

Mikhail took the key and shackle. "Come."

Severn re-sheathed his blade and approached Mikhail. "I'm not leaving you alone with him."

Solo stayed kneeling, wishing he could shrink into a tiny ball and hide.

"Solo, return to your chamber," Mikhail said. "We will discuss all of this when I return."

"Yes, Your Grace." He couldn't look at any of them, not even Luxen, and swiftly dove off the side of Aerie's dome, spiraling downward toward his balcony.

How had it all gone so wrong? He'd only wanted to fix things, not make them worse, but somehow he'd gotten tangled up in things he didn't understand, like emotions, and now he didn't know what was right and what was... lies. Had Luxen used his allure? It would explain why Solo reacted physically to the demon. And why he'd lost control like he had. The kissing. The... other thing, Luxen making him come.

Shame sweated from his skin. He paced his chamber, wings trailing.

He'd thought Luxen had wanted *him*. Not his ether, *him*. He'd been a fool, just as he'd feared. Luxen had even told him how he manipulated to survive. He must have been laughing at Solo the entire time they'd been chained together.

Solo was a joke.

It hurt. His chest hurt, his heart hurt, everything hurt.

He knelt and folded his wings around himself, hiding inside. It hurt, but he had no wound to mend. If this was what caring and emotions did to you, then he wanted none of them.

He wanted to go home, his *real* home, to the tiny house and many cats. Hopefully they hadn't abandoned him.

"Solo?"

Oh Seraphim, Mikhail was here. Mikhail had been through so much. He'd learned to love and feel and care, but Solo wasn't as strong as him. Solo had to face him but he couldn't stand to see the disappointment on his face. He unfolded his wings and looked up.

Mikhail knelt on one knee and laid his wings low on either side of him. He rested his arm over his knee. His face spoke of pity, of his own hurt. "I know how difficult it is, but it's going to be all right. You'll make it through."

"I thought..." Solo's voice caught in his throat. "Never mind. It doesn't matter. I'm sorry I failed you."

"We should never have put you in charge of Luxen's incarceration, knowing how... capable he is of using our weaknesses against us. I understand. He... Well, I know what it's like to have Luxen's power blinding you to the truth."

"But... it didn't feel like lies." If he'd been bespelled, had Luxen's allure controlling him, wouldn't he have at least sensed some wrongness?

"That's what makes him so dangerous." Mikhail smiled sympathetically. "Rest a while. Luxen is back in the enclosure. Severn is looking for Samiel. Try to move on."

Solo nodded, unsure how to move on, but if Mikhail had, then he had to try. As the guardian angel turned away, one thought crossed his mind. "Mikhail, what will happen to Luxen?"

"I fear he is too dangerous to be freed."

But they couldn't keep him locked up forever, that was cruel. Unless... "You mean to kill him?" he whispered.

Mikhail's wings sagged as he sighed. "He has sealed his fate."

Solo stared after him long after he'd flown from the balcony. The drapes rippled in the breeze and sometimes, from outside, distant laughter from dancing angels and demons sounded.

It wasn't right. Even if Luxen had manipulated Solo, he didn't deserve to be killed.

The pup afraid of stars.

Solo fought back tears.

Had angels changed at all?

CHAPTER 10

*L*uxen

THERE WAS a new angel on guard outside the enclosure, not Solomon. This guard did not bring him sandwiches with the crusts cut off, he didn't talk, and he was not as pleasant to watch as Solomon.

Nobody came for days. Samiel's enclosure remained empty. And Luxen paced.

It felt different this time.

A sword hung over his neck, ready to fall. He was not afraid to die. It was better Solo never knew the truth— that Luxen hadn't used his allure on the angel, and never would. His death wouldn't hurt Solomon, if Solomon believed Luxen the villain. He'd probably be relieved.

When had he begun to care about an angel's feelings? Perhaps from the first moment those scarlet wings had flared in front of him, standing between him and

Konstantin, between Luxen and death. But it didn't matter now. Wasn't it ironic how in these final hours, he believed the impossible? A demon could care for an angel.

Only one though. Only Solomon.

At least, if this was to be Luxen's end, he'd gotten to see the bliss on the angel's face the moment he'd let go of himself and spilled his pent-up desire. It was no surprise Konstantin had arrived after that; the blast of Solomon's ether had almost knocked Luxen out cold, and that hadn't happened since he'd been a pup, unable to absorb too much ether. Solomon was an inferno, Luxen had been right in that. He chuckled about it now, enjoying how the memory warmed his veins and aroused his cock. If Solomon had been his, he'd have worshipped him day and night. Make him come a thousand times, whatever he needed.

Perhaps it was for the best that it would never happen.

The enclosure's outer door rattled and Konstantin entered—wings illusioned away.

Luxen drew himself up to his full height, wings too. "Come to gloat, High Lord?"

Konstantin stopped in the middle of the viewing area and stared at the empty enclosure next to Luxen's. "I'd ask you where he is but I can't trust the answer."

"You think you can't trust *me*?" Luxen braced a forearm against the glass and peered through its warped thickness. "Says the demon who lied with his every breath for ten years to the angels, and to himself."

Konstantin sneered, his upper lip rippling in a snarl. "Why did it have to be Solo?"

Luxen shrugged. "Why not? You put him here. I was

bored. I couldn't fuck him, but I could fuck with him. What else was I supposed to do?"

Konstantin lunged and slammed a massive hand against the enclosure's glass. The glass rattled but held. "Not touch him! Solo's not for you to fuck with!"

Luxen hadn't even flinched. "Maybe that should be his choice?"

"Choice? You didn't give him a choice. Your allure was all over him. He didn't stand a fucking chance, exactly like you did to Mikhail!"

Konstantin's rage was real, so real it stole Luxen's breath and his voice, just for a moment. Luxen wasn't going to win this. He hadn't used any kind of allure on Solomon, but Konstantin would never believe him. How his allure was all over Solomon, he had no idea. Perhaps it was his scent, and Konstantin was confused. Blinded by an old anger that forever festered between them.

"How is he?" Luxen asked. He wanted—needed to know Solomon would be okay.

Konstantin blinked and backed up. "Mikhail tells me he's... He will be all right. He's vulnerable, like all angels are when they realize everything they've known has been a lie. You took advantage of that. If there was any reason to end you, that alone would be enough."

"So I am to be ended?"

At Konstantin's sigh, his wings shimmered back into sight and sagged behind him. "I had hoped the killing was over, but we can make one last exception for you, Luxen." He faced him, inches from the glass. "After what you did to Mikhail and now Solo, I'll be glad of it."

Luxen had nothing to add. He wasn't going to apologize for trying to save demonkind. And what did he do to

Mikhail that was so terrible? Made him look in a fucking mirror to see the monster he truly was?

They shared a moment of silence, simmering over with hatred, and then Konstantin left, slamming the door behind him.

So be it.

Luxen should have died as a pup long ago. This had been a long time coming.

A jagged crack in the glass caught his eye.

He reached up and picked at it with a sharp nail. It hadn't been there before. When Konstantin had hit the glass, he must have weakened it.

Luxen spread his palm over the crack and a soft puff of air tickled his skin.

He smiled. Maybe it wasn't over just yet.

CHAPTER 11

*S*olo

Five was still missing. Solo had called her name, earning some funny looks from his human neighbors. He'd left a tin of her favorite tuna out, but that had only attracted another cat. He didn't know what else to do. Maybe he wasn't a good enough caretaker, and she'd decided to leave?

He fed the others, their tails springing and wobbling in the air with their heads in the bowls, and feeling as though he'd been run over by several emotional busses, he retreated to the shower. Could water wash off shame and guilt?

Warm water rained over him. He lathered his hair with bubbles, then slid soap over his arms, and chest, where Luxen's hands had stroked. He'd had soft hands, for a demon. But his nails had been sharp. His teeth too. Solo poked at the cut in his lip with his tongue and a zip of sizzling lust travelled all the way down his back and into his hardening cock.

Cock.

That's what demons called it. He'd asked Severn, who had then gone on to say all sorts of names humans had for the male member. Cock sounded better than member.

And now he had his *cock* in his hand, and while his fingers were smaller and slimmer than Luxen's, all he had to do was close his eyes and imagine it was Luxen's hand pumping. His body knew exactly what to do and with his head full of Luxen, he allowed himself the release, gasping as he came, shuddering and spilling. There had been a time that doing such a thing would have gotten an angel thrown in Haven, shut away from the world.

Water washed away the milky seed, and with it what little pleasure he'd gotten. He still felt hollow.

When would they kill Luxen?

Should he go to him or would that make everything worse?

What if he was already dead?

Solo almost sobbed at that last thought but shored himself up with a deep, steadying breath. He had to see Luxen. Had to talk to him. Back behind the glass, he'd tell Solo the truth now, and Solo needed to know if it had all been a lie.

He left the shower, towel dried, threw on loose-fitting linens to save time, and fled his house for the sky, barely slamming the front door closed before his boots left the ground. The abandoned zoo was adjacent to old Regents Park in a section of London decimated by war. The scar was a black patch in London's twinkling skyline. He beat his wings, his resolve growing. He'd speak to Luxen and he'd know, for certain, if the demon had been using him. Beyond the deal they'd already struck. And if he was, well, Solo might kill him himself.

He landed on the overgrown pathway outside the exotic animal enclosures and jogged down the steps. The new guard was sitting slumped on the bottom step. Asleep?

No... not asleep.

"Oh no..." Solo checked the angel's neck and found a steady pulse. Not dead, unconscious. The door to the enclosures hung open, just like it had before. Solo already knew what he wouldn't find inside—*who* he wouldn't find. Sure enough, Luxen's enclosure was empty, its glass shattered, pieces glittering on the ground.

Damn him. But could Solo blame him?

Mikhail had to know.

He flew to Aerie, alerted a healer to the unconscious guard, and hurried to Mikhail's chamber. Outside, he raised a fist to knock, and hesitated. What if Mikhail thought Solo had done this? He wouldn't. Mikhail trusted him... but he believed Solo to be under Luxen's allure. And an angel who had been compromised *would* free Luxen. All the more reason to tell him now, before news reached him by other means.

Solo chewed on his bottom lip and stepped back from the door.

Or he could... not tell him.

He was not supposed to be involved. He'd have to admit he'd gone there to speak with Luxen, going against a direct order not to.

He should walk away.

Luxen had escaped, and that wasn't anything to do with him.

Except, he knew where Luxen was.

The knowledge came to him without a shred of doubt. Because he knew Luxen, knew how his mind worked. He wouldn't go back to the demons, no... That would be too obvious. Instead, he'd hide in plain sight.

Solo backed away from Mikhail's door, almost falling over his own wings in his haste. His heart did a strange little hopeful leap, which he ignored, should it be the allure messing with him.

Of course, Solo might be very wrong. But as he raced through Aerie, trying to keep from running to avoid attracting attention, he knew he was right. In the central chamber, he glanced up, trying to see the hidden crevice between the domes, but the light reflected back, blinding him. Luxen wasn't up there. Severn would look there.

No, Solo knew exactly where to find him.

He dropped off the edge of the central disk and climbed through the air, circling around to the residential disk, then he descended, gave his wings a soft flutter, and landed silently on his own balcony. The doors were closed. He tried the handle, eased it down, and the door popped open. Solo crept inside. The lights were off. Shadows layered the bed, the resting area. The door to the bathroom hung open.

He listened, but nothing seemed out of place.

Perhaps he *had* been wrong.

He'd been convinced—

A shadow launched from the dark. Solo ducked, flattening his wings, and jerked his elbow up, sinking it into his attacker's middle to flip him over his head. But the attacker had wings too, and threw them open like parachutes, filling the ceiling with their leathery expanse. Luxen landed in a crouch, wings arched behind him, and growled.

"Wait, it's me!" Solo cried. "I'm not here to hurt you. Unless you make me."

The growling stopped. "Solomon?"

"Yes." He almost laughed. He *had* been right.

Luxen straightened, folded his wings, and started forward. "What are you doing here?"

"This is *my* chamber." Now he did laugh. "I knew you'd be here."

Luxen stopped in front of him, bare-chested and mean-looking, his expression severe. "Did you come alone?" He glanced toward the balcony doors.

"First, answer my question. Did you seduce me with your allure?"

A muscle in Luxen's jaw twitched. "It would make both our lives easier if I had."

He wasn't lying.

Relief made Solo's heart soar. It had been real! All of it!

Luxen smiled. His warm hand was on Solo's cheek, and he had moved so close his heat burned through Solo's clothes. In the dark, Luxen's eyes glowed. His nails dragged down Solo's cheek, on the sweet side of pain.

"You shouldn't be here," Solo whispered.

"Which is exactly why I am. Will you give me up? Have them take me away?"

"I should." Solo lifted onto his tiptoes and flexed his wings behind him. He folded his arms over Luxen's shoulders and pulled the demon down so their mouths almost touched. "If I was a good angel, I would have already told Mikhail."

"So why haven't you?"

Solo pinched Luxen's bottom lip between his teeth and let it spring free. "Because I'm not a good angel."

A growling purr rumbled through Luxen. "On the contrary." His hands scorched Solo's hips and Luxen guided him backward. "I think you're *very* good."

Oh, this was happening. Luxen was backing Solo toward the bed, his eyes aglow with want, his wings stretched high behind him. Solo's heart raced. A demon wanted him. A powerful concubi demon. The thought alone had Solo's skin flushing hot and every feather extending.

Luxen's strong, confident hand hooked around Solo's lower back. He bent Solo against him and nuzzled his neck. "Hm... It's not allure... It's something else... Something we spark."

Solo didn't care what it was; he clutched Luxen to him, needing more of it. More of the demon. All over him. "I touched myself."

Luxen's lips teased his ear, spilling shivers down Solo's neck. "You did?"

"Thinking of you."

A deep, thunder-like growl rumbled through Luxen. When Solo turned his head, the demon's eyes burned. "Did you come?" Luxen asked.

"I did."

He scooped Solo up by the ass so fast that his head spun, and threw him down onto the soft bed.

Solo grinned and propped himself on his elbows to watch the demon loom over him. He was breathtaking, with his proud horns, his wings like works of art, his body a feast. Solo would never get enough of just staring and admiring and absorbing *all that*.

"Are your clothes important to you?" Luxen asked, his voice already wrecked.

"What?"

Luxen growled, clutched Solo's linen shirt, and tore the slip of fabric clean down the middle.

"Oh."

If there had been any protest to voice, it was lost the moment the demon's hot hands touched his chest and Luxen's wet mouth closed around a nipple. Solo arched, hooked a leg around Luxen's thigh, and moaned a sound he hadn't known he could make.

"Your ether..." Luxen panted. "I have to absorb it. Forgive me. I can't resist you."

"Take it." He folded both legs around the back of Luxen's, trapping him close. "Take *me*."

Luxen cupped his face, stroked his hair, and bowed his forehead to touch Solo's. "I can't."

Solo must have misheard. "What?"

"I can't... do this."

What was he saying? "Did I..."

Luxen pushed up onto both hands, his expression so pained that it hurt Solo to see it. He went to his knees, forcing Solo to free him.

"Did I do something wrong?"

"No..."

Solo caught his hand before he could pull away completely and pressed it to his chest, over his heart. "You feel that?"

Luxen's smile slid sideways. "It races."

"For you, for this. Don't stop. I don't know what I'm doing, but I want it—*this*."

"You don't know what you want."

Was the demon lord ashamed? But that could not be... Unless... someone had warned him off. Mikhail? No. Severn... Yes, Severn would threaten Luxen. He was Solo's friend, but he did not speak for Solo. "You think I'm fragile? Do you think I'm some confused little angel who doesn't understand the sex?"

"Solomo—"

He did! The fact he tried to pull away proved it. "No. I may not understand any of this but I've spent my whole life fearing it, and I'll not have you or anyone else tell me what I do and do not want."

Luxen bowed his head.

Oh no... This wasn't fair. Solo scrabbled to his knees to face Luxen, almost eye to eye, although he had to look up to meet his gaze. "I want this." He cupped the demon's thick cock through his trousers. "And I want this." He kissed him like they'd kissed the first time, full of fury and desperation. Luxen opened, rocking with him, breathing with him, clutching at him. And when the kiss ended, Luxen panted against Solo's lips and his body trembled against Solo's.

Solo grabbed his left horn. "And I want you."

Luxen clutched at Solo's neck, his fingers so thick they cradled the back of his head too. "You don't know what it is you're asking. You're angel. I'm concubi." He hauled Solo close and snarled, "I could kill you."

It wasn't a threat. It came from a place of fear too.

Solo locked his hand in Luxen's hair and twisted. "You won't."

CHAPTER 12

Luxen

THIS ANGEL WOULD BE the death of him, if not via Konstantin's wrath, then by Luxen's own foolishness to fall for him so deeply and completely that he might just do anything for him. Solomon's heart beat like a drum, his body so tantalizing he might never tire of touching it. He bowed his head and licked Solomon's shoulder—tasting it, tasting him. Solo thrummed, trembling, panting, his wings a canvas of red in the air, his hair a fiery mess, eyes shining like emeralds, and lips, soft, wet, and sweet like peaches. Luxen wanted to touch and taste it all. But the very last thing he wanted was to hurt him. And the risk was real. Despite being smaller than most concubi, Luxen was still larger than angels, in every way.

Solomon didn't know what he was asking. He knew his

desires, he knew what he wanted, but there was a difference between wanting and knowing.

Kneeling, eye to eye, Solomon was aflame, a creature so beautiful Luxen was afraid he'd burn up and vanish, because this could not be happening. He didn't care for angels. He wanted to fuck them, but that was the concubi way. What he wanted with Solo was so much more. So fierce, this one. So full of fiery strength. Luxen couldn't resist.

Luxen took his free hand and teased his fingers through Solomon's red hair. Solomon tilted his head, leaning into the touch. His lashes fluttered down, his eyes closed, and Luxen wondered if he'd ever seen something so precious. And how had it come to this—to him falling for an angel.

Solomon's small hands pressed to Luxen's bare chest. He opened his eyes and peered up. The smattering of freckles across his nose were dark against his flushed skin. He smiled, shyly. "You don't need to be afraid of me."

Luxen would have laughed had any other angel said those words, but somehow, Solomon's words found that vulnerable chink in Luxen's armor and worked their way inside to the small pup-like part of him that had hidden from stars. He believed him. Luxen brushed his lips over Solomon's, so lightly they barely touched. The angel parted for him; his wet tongue flicked in, seeking Luxen's. Even this, a simple kiss, felt precious. Ether rippled and washed through and over Luxen, making his wings ache and his cock throb.

Once he fell, there would be no return.

Was he brave enough to love an angel? Because it changed *everything*.

The ghost of a kiss quickly heated, with Solomon's fire driving his passion. He burned in Luxen's arms, writhing close, and when the kiss broke apart, his mouth trailed down Luxen's neck, blunt teeth nipping, while his hands kneaded and stroked, sliding down Luxen's back to cup his ass and grind closer. He growled at himself to keep from breaking apart and roughly pounding the angel into his soft, fluffy pillows. Then Solomon's flighty hands dove to Luxen's cock, unlaced his pants, and suddenly the angel stopped and stared, his head bowed, wings flexing with his heavy breaths.

Luxen couldn't see his face, just the back of his head, but he could imagine what he was thinking. A demon cock was no small thing and while Solomon had felt its bulge, he hadn't seen it, hadn't *touched* it.

"Oh..."

Luxen gritted his teeth and stroked Solomon's hair. His small hands still had a firm grip on his dick, and if Solomon didn't move them soon, Luxen might combust on the spot.

He should probably say something to alleviate his fears, to reassure him, but he feared any word that fell from his lips would sound like a growl and frighten him.

"Well..."

Solomon looked up, his smirk slanted, and with both hands, he began to stroke Luxen's cock.

Words were no longer an option. Instead, Luxen slid his hand under Solomon's hair and rested it against the back of his neck and leaned back, face tipped toward the ceiling. Lubricant wasn't an issue. Solomon had already gathered the pre-cum under his thumb and slid it down Luxen's length. Luxen garbled a growl and a moan, then

Solomon's mouth sealed around his nipple and the angel's little tongue lapped.

Delicious spiked darts of pleasure danced through him, turning his skin molten. Ether rolled over him. It was bliss. It was basking in sunlight, it was flying as high and as fast as he ever had, it was racing through thunderclouds, skimming the ocean, it was everything that had ever made his heart soar. It was Solo.

Luxen wanted to take his own cock and enter him, hold his wings and fuck him from behind, but Solomon needed care, needed love. For all his talk of want, his body wasn't ready, not for Luxen.

He folded his arm around Solo's back and pulled him down, over him, so Luxen lay beneath him with Solo on top. Solo's great wings arched high, filling the space above them, their feathered tips skimming the ceiling. Luxen lost himself in watching how the soft light spilling in from the balcony doors set each feather on fire, but then Solo slunk downward, and his tongue lapped at Luxen's cockhead. Luxen dug his nails into the bed and gripped the sheets, because if he got his hands on Solo, he'd hurt him.

Light fingers encircled his girth, and Solo's warm, wet mouth sealed around his erection. Luxen writhed, his legs trapped under Solo's ass, his cock at the angel's mercy.

And that was how he learned that Solo, Angel of Aerie, was not merciful.

CHAPTER 13

Solo

HE'D NEVER FELT a thrill like it. Luxen was spread under him, his wings sprawled either side, draping off the bed, his body splayed for the taking. His muscular chest gleamed, his powerful thighs shifted under Solo's weight, but his cock... It was so thick it almost didn't fit in Solo's mouth, and when Luxen moaned and growled and grabbed the sheets like if he didn't hold on to something, he might fall, Solo wanted nothing else in that moment than to make him come. But not fast, oh no. The writhing and the moaning sounds were good sounds. He liked this. A lot. So Solo worshipped the thick, twitching length with his tongue and lips. Sometimes, he came up to breathe and blew on the veined, wet length, prompting a strange growling mew from Luxen.

There was so much joy to be had in pleasuring Luxen

that his own needy cock was easily ignored. Although a brush against Luxen's thigh, every now and then, reminded him how hard he was.

"I need..." Luxen garbled.

Solo lifted off and peered up the length of the demon's amazing body, his chin resting against the side of Luxen's cock. "What do you need?"

"I need you in me."

Solo blinked. Right. The sex. Well, part of it. The main part, he supposed. He wasn't sure though... how it worked. He knew the logistics, where things went, but Luxen wasn't a seraphim, or an angel. Everything was... bigger.

"Fuck me, Solo."

Oh. Solo's wings twitched, his heart constricted, and his cock leaped, spilling tiny strands of silky pre-cum on Luxen's thigh. The fuck was the same as the sex?

Luxen smiled and crooked a finger. Solo prowled up his body, planting a knee either side of his hip, and braced over him. He had Luxen pinned, at his mercy. He could taste his saltiness, could feel his heat, and when he flexed his cock, it touched Luxen's belly, making the demon's eyes shine. Solo tilted his hips, sliding his cock up Luxen's hip —it felt too good.

"You like that... Now imagine that feeling, but wrapped in muscle, my muscle... Imagine driving yourself into me, Solo."

Yes, he could do that. He shuddered, moved his hips some more, rubbing harder.

"When you touched yourself, do you remember how tight your fingers were? You pumped hard, Solo. So hard that your body took over. You fucked your hand and you came." Luxen parted his thighs. "Do that, in me."

"Yes..." Solo needed it *now*. Rearing up, he gripped Luxen's hips, shifting his angle to expose Luxen's ass and the tight crevice between his cheeks. Luxen spread his legs wide. His cock lay heavy against his belly, his balls low, and beneath that, the hole that Solo was supposed to *enter*.

"Look at me."

He looked up, heart pounding in his throat.

Luxen breathed hard but he wasn't angry or frustrated. His horns gleamed. His grin twitched. "You won't hurt me. Do what you want, what your body already knows. Fuck me. Fuck me like you crave. Fuck me until you lose your mind. Come in me, Solo. Come hard, fill me up, take me as you want."

His mind cleared. He did want this. He wasn't sure what it was exactly, but Luxen was right, his body knew. Solo stroked his fingers down Luxen's wet cock, sliding them lower and then circling the hole, slicking it. He shifted forward on his knees, took his own cock, lined it up with the hole, and pushed. A unique tingle teased up his spine, and as the constricted ring of muscle gave way and took him in, the tingle grew, driving him on, urging him deeper. Yes, this was it. He wasn't there yet, but he wanted this, chased it.

"Deeper," Luxen growled, hands twisting in the sheets.

Solo snarled and thrust. The tingle snapped, blinding him, riding him. He gasped and braced against Luxen's heaving chest. More. He needed more. He withdrew, the muscle caressing him, and thrust again. "Oh Seraphim..."

"Yes, angel. *Yes. Fuck me deeper.*"

Again, Solo thrust, slapping his hips against the underside of Luxen's thighs. No, the angle was wrong. He could get deeper still, if he just... He hooked one of Luxen's legs over his shoulder, shifting him, opening him, and slammed in. Luxen moaned. His thick cock jumped, leaking silky seed, and Solo dug his fingers into Luxen's hip while the other hand clamped his leg at his shoulder. Yes... this. This was the sex. This was the fucking, and he *wanted it all*.

"Harder, Solo. Lose yourself and fuck me, angel!"

He thrust, withdrew, thrust harder. Skin slapped on skin, his cock turned to slick heat, and with every pump into Luxen, he chased a tantalizing ecstasy, building and building, until there was no more Solo, just the fucking. He grabbed Luxen's twitching cock and jerked it, pleasuring him as he pistoned into Luxen's hole.

Luxen's breaths came fast and jagged. His cock was wet, so thick and hard, like oiled steel. Solo wanted to suck it, but that thought made his own member throb, needing more. He pumped harder. Luxen growled for more, demanded to be fucked harder, and Solo answered his demands until his body ran with sweat and his wings sagged, trembling.

The tingling raced to a crescendo beginning in his lower back, the pressure building. He was going to come, but he didn't want to—not yet. By Seraphim, it was happening, and he couldn't stop it.

"Yes, Solo." Luxen arched, his cock driving deep into Solo's wet fist. He shuddered, cried out, and his own creamy seed spurted up his chest.

That was it, that was the moment Solo lost all control. He grabbed Luxen's hips in both hands, adjusting the angle, and fucked him hard, fucked him deep, fucked him until his whole body sang and his wings burned and his soul burst into flames. He moaned, teetering on the edge of ecstasy, and came like lightning, spilling in jagged, messy thrusts, seeking to plunge his seed deep into some hidden part of Luxen.

He looked down at where his cock was buried in Luxen's body, the joining of angel and demon, and the fluttering of his heart came from joy, not shame or anguish.

"Solo?" Luxen growled. "Are you all right?"

"Yes." He grinned. "Let's do it again."

***

THEY HAD DONE the sex again, on the bed and in the shower, with their wings hidden, no less frantic each time. But in all of it, Solo thought this moment was the best, with Luxen on the bed, on his side, snoring lightly. He seemed smaller somehow, although he wasn't. But tucked close, his wings draped out of the way behind him, a sheet slung over his lower half, he didn't look like the ex-High Lord who had tried to turn Mikhail against them, the formidable demon High Lord who had sent his kin into battle with angels.

He just looked like Luxen—a demon. Like any other who had tried to survive against worsening odds. He had done terrible things. But so had Mikhail. So had Severn; so even had Solo, on the battlefield.

Killing Luxen wasn't right.

By now, the others would have learned Luxen was missing from the enclosure.

They'd come, eventually arriving at Solo's chamber when they realized he wasn't at home.

What if he took Luxen and flew away somewhere?

Hm, but there were the cats to consider. They'd adopted Solo. He couldn't abandon them.

If they left, they'd be forever checking the skies. Luxen would be hunted. And Solo wasn't sure he could live with that, even if Luxen could. There had to be a way to make Mikhail and Severn see how Luxen wasn't bad. If he went to them, they'd have to listen. It had been a few days; they'd think the allure had worn off. They'd hear him this time.

Solo crept from the bed, making sure not to wake Luxen, dressed in his angel clothes—loose linens—buttoned his waistcoat, laced his boots, and slipped from the room without making a sound. With any luck, he'd be back before Luxen woke.

He walked through Aerie's airy corridors, passing angels and a handful of demons. It was late, or early, he wasn't sure, but Aerie was quiet. Until he reached the central chamber. Angels bustled around. A few, he spotted clipping angelblades to their hips.

Oh no...

He stopped an angel and asked, "What's happened?"

"A demon killed an angel."

Dread hollowed his gut. "What? Who?"

"You should see Mikhail. He'll want you on this, General Solomon."

"Yes. Where is he?"

"In the council room. With Konstantin."

Solo nodded and hurried toward the stairs that would take him down to the council chambers. The sight that greeted him inside was one he thought he'd never see again. Mikhail, in demon leathers, and Severn beside him, an angelblade broadsword sheathed at his hip.

"Ah, General..." Severn greeted him. "Sorry to wake you so late."

"What? Yes," he stammered. They'd sent someone to his house, it seemed. Thankfully, that person hadn't reported back yet or they might have been knocking on his chamber door next.

Demons and angels stood around the long council table, one demon being the formidable Djall, Konstantin's sister. She looked through Solomon, eyeing him as though wondering which part of him she'd devour first if she could get close enough to slice pieces off.

"What's going on?"

"You weren't told?"

"I... It's... I just... I don't quite believe it."

"Indeed," Mikhail said soberly. "But it's true. An angel has been killed. We have a witness." He let the silence fall before adding, "It was Luxen."

Solo somehow managed to keep his wings from bursting open and blurting out the thousands of denials filling his head. But he couldn't rush to defend Luxen when they still believed Solo compromised. "When and where did this happen?" he demanded.

"At the enclosure. Luxen escaped and killed the guard charged with watching him."

But that guard had been alive when Solo had left him. "I... don't think that's quite right. If I may explain... I alerted the healers to the wounded guard after discovering Luxen was missing myself, earlier in the evening."

Murmurs simmered about the table. Glances were exchanged. His credibility had been eroded before, and now more of it crumbled away.

"I went there to speak with him," he added.

Mikhail's expression darkened.

"It's not what you think."

Severn shook his head. "Solo—"

"Hear me out." Solo spoke with just enough anger to silence them. "I went there to speak with him, yes, but he wasn't there. He'd already escaped. The guard was alive. I checked him myself. I immediately returned to Aerie and sent the healers down to him."

"He was dead when they arrived," Severn said, his voice flat. He couldn't believe Solo had anything to do with this?

"Not possible. He was unconscious, but otherwise unharmed. How did he die?"

"Blade to the chest."

Solo gasped. "Well then, as terrible as this is, Luxen wasn't there, and after he'd left, the angel was alive. He didn't do this. Someone must have returned and killed him."

"You sound very sure," Severn said.

"I'm stating facts."

"Why would someone do that?" Mikhail asked, his tone not as hard as Severn's but still piqued with suspicion.

"I don't know."

Mikhail's wings lifted. "Why didn't you come to me with this?"

Solo swallowed. "I almost did, I just... You believe I'm compromised and I didn't want to get involved. I thought it better if I... returned home. To the cats." Which had been his plan, until he'd realized where Luxen would be hiding out.

"You left an angel to die?" Djall asked. "That's cold, even for an angel."

Feathers ruffled, angels bristling.

"No, that's not what happened," Solo denied. "Were

you listening? He was fine, just unconscious. I sent healers—"

"Could it be you missed a wound to the chest, Solomon?" Djall asked, eyebrow raised.

None of the council members believed him. None would even look him in the eye. "No. I did not miss a wound to the chest. I'm a veteran of the war, the same as you. I am more than familiar with battle wounds, Djall."

"Well, we might be more inclined to believe you if you weren't tainted by Luxen." This came from Mikhail.

Solo clenched his jaw. "Your Grace, I'm not—"

"And we have a witness who says they saw Luxen leaving the enclosure with an angelblade," Mikhail added.

Lies! "Your witness is mistaken," Solo hissed.

"Do you know where Luxen is, Solo?" Severn asked.

Solo met Severn's gaze. His friend. His brother-in-arms. They'd been through much. Fought side by side in battle. Solo had saved Severn's life, and Severn his, time and time again. For all their differences, Solo counted Severn among one of only two people he would die for. But in this, Severn was wrong. "No," Solo lied.

"Your Grace." Severn turned to Mikhail. "We must lockdown Aerie. I know Luxen. The last thing he wants is peace between angels and demons. He will come for you. Where he failed before, he'll try again—"

"You don't know that," Solo interrupted. His heart might pound from his chest at any second if nobody started listening to him.

Severn raised a hand. "With respect, General, you don't know him like I do. He has already proven he will kill for this. And he's armed."

Solo pulled his wings in, folded his arms, and bit his tongue. Anger sizzled the back of his throat.

"Agreed," Mikhail said.

Solo couldn't listen to this. To their blind hatred and prejudice. Did they even hear themselves? This was exactly how things had been before. "You're making a mistake."

"No, Luxen did that, when he killed the guard and manipulated you," Severn said. "If I'd had any leniency in me, it's gone." He scanned the lords and angels around the table. "Luxen is to be killed on sight."

The words cut through Solo's heart. No. *No, this was wrong!* "I never thought you'd disappoint me. Both of you."

Mikhail frowned. "Solo, you're compromised and emotional."

He slammed a fist onto the table, rattling its entire length and setting the demons and angels aflutter. *"What I am is right! But none of you will listen!"*

They stared. And he knew how he sounded, how he looked.

With a growl, he turned on his heel.

"General Solomon," Severn growled. "We need you in this."

"No, you don't." Solo left the chamber and climbed the stairs two steps at a time. He had to get to Luxen *fast*. Once Aerie was locked down, no angel or demon could fly in or out without approval. Luxen would be trapped in Aerie, in a nest of killers, just as he'd feared. He should be scared of stars, Solo realized. Because they were coming for him.

CHAPTER 14

*L*uxen

CHUCKLING LAUGHTER WOKE HIM. *Demon* laughter. Luxen squinted into the gloom, trying to make sense of the shadows and his unfamiliar surroundings. *Solo...* The bed beside him was empty, the sheets ruffled. An angel's bed. He rubbed at his forehead, beneath his right horn. An ether overload had left his thoughts fogged and his body wrecked, in the best way, but something was wrong.

He wasn't alone.

"Things I thought I'd never see... Lord Luxen drunk on angel, in an angel's bed."

Samiel.

Instincts cleared some of the fog in Luxen's head. He focused on the hulking shape of demon moving through the shadows at the far end of the chamber. Samiel picked up some porcelain trinket of Solo's and examined it in his clawed hands—a small porcelain cat. "Hm..." His thick fingers squeezed, and the trinket shattered. "Oops."

"Samiel..." Luxen croaked. Why was he here? Had he taken Solo? Where was Solo? "What's going on?"

"You know, when a *friend* told me he'd seen you in the skies above Aerie, I said no, that's not possible. Luxen would never fly with angels. But here you are, fucking one."

Samiel's words were clipped, sharp with restrained anger. The demon had been passionate about defending themselves, as all demons were. But Samiel had been loyal to Luxen through it all. So much so that he'd lied to his lifelong friend Konstantin for Luxen, for the cause.

His rage at finding Luxen in an angel's bed wasn't difficult to figure out. Samiel's being here could not end well for anyone. Luxen slid his legs from the bed and pulled on his trousers, discreetly searching for any kind of weapon should Samiel's anger boil over into something more physical. He'd been able to order Samiel around before, but things had changed. Luxen was no longer High Lord. They were equal. No, not equal. Samiel was *above* Luxen; his prowess in battle and his size made it so.

Luxen crossed the floor and met Samiel in the middle of the room. He kept his wings high, higher than Samiel's. His wings, at least, were bigger. "Samiel, you need to leave. If you're found here, they'll kill you."

Samiel shrugged a shoulder and wing. "Maybe. Did you think this happy little union was going to last?" He circled his finger in the air. "Did you think I was going to let you just... fly away after what you did *to me*?"

"Samiel, we did what was necessary at the time. Perhaps... we were wrong."

Samiel bared his teeth. "I followed my High Lord's orders! I did everything ordered of me. I bowed down to your fucking rule, Luxen. I betrayed Konstantin *for you*."

"For the cause. Not for me."

Samiel snorted. "The cause?" He laughed and circled around, thick muscles quivering. "Here's how it's going to be... Right now, the angels are losing their shit because Lord Luxen has escaped and killed one of them. Oh no, so terrible. They'd already decided we were going to die, but instead of leaving us in that rat-infested glass tank to rot, they're now going to hunt—"

Luxen grabbed the fool by the neck and hauled him off his feet. *"What did you do?!"*

Samiel's wings flapped. His feet dangled. He clawed at Luxen's grip. But then something in him changed. He quit struggling and smiled. "They all want you dead," he croaked. "Including your pretty little red one."

Solo?

No.

Solo wouldn't. "Lies."

"Where is he then, hm? Why isn't he here?"

"You don't know anything." Luxen threw him away. Samiel caught himself in the air with a few flaps and landed.

"They called him back, told him what you've done, and now he's coming here to kill you, Luxen. They all want you dead."

Luxen laughed. The others maybe, but not Solo. "Just go. Whatever you've planned, I don't want any part of it."

"It's too late for that. You're right in the middle of it. You think I'll stop at killing one angel to smear your already tainted name? They don't need an excuse to hunt you down, but I'll give them plenty. It's not hard to find angels who want war, who will say they saw you, because they know Lord Luxen should pay for all the angels his demons have killed in battle."

Samiel was proving to be more of a problem than Luxen had thought him capable of. If what he was saying was true, then he'd maneuvered Luxen into an impossible position. Samiel had given the angels the evidence they needed to condemn him. Konstantin alone would kill Luxen on a whim. But now Luxen had angel blood on his hands, Konstantin would cut him down in the name of justice and order all the angels to do the same. Demons too, probably. If Mikhail ordered Solo to kill Luxen... he might just do it.

"There it is," Samiel said. "The moment he realizes he's trapped."

"Very clever, Samiel. I underestimated you." Luxen hadn't thought him capable, but the evidence was right in front of him.

"And you ruined *my life*." He ruffled his leathery wings, reining in his anger. "Leave with me now. It's the only way you survive."

Leave Solo? The idea cinched his heart. "Then what? What is your plan, Samiel? Are we to hide forever?"

"There are others, like us... Others who see this sham peace for what it is—a smokescreen for angels taking over."

Just a few days ago, he wouldn't have hesitated. But things had changed. Luxen had changed. He was no longer sure what he believed. But he had begun to realize that real peace might be possible. That it might even be worth fighting for.

The balcony doors flew open. Solo landed inside, wings rippling. "Luxen, we have to—" He saw Samiel and froze. "What the...?"

Samiel growled. "Hello, *angel*."

Solo roared, and lunged.

CHAPTER 15

Solo

HE TWISTED and slammed his shoulder into Samiel. He had to act fast. Unarmed, speed and agility were his only advantage against Samiel's bulk and muscle. It wouldn't be enough, not unless Solo dropped him in seconds. The demon rocked backward but dug his heels in and surged like a tidal wave. Luxen yelled something, but the words were lost behind Samiel's answering roar. Solo clenched his hand into a fist to bring it down on Samiel's cheek, but the demon's right hook slammed into his gut, punching him backward. Air tore from his lungs. His body buckled. He flung out his wings to keep from falling and stumbled to his feet. Sudden wetness soaked his shirt. He clutched his chest, startled to find his hand came away glistening with blood.

A bloody angelblade glinted in Samiel's hand.

The blood on Solo's hand... He struggled to correlate one with the other.

Luxen rushed in. Strong arms came around Solo. He smelled demon, and warmth rushed over him. "Solo..." Luxen's hand cupped Solo's face.

No, Luxen couldn't be here. Mikhail, Severn, they were coming! He shoved at the demon. "Go."

"Healers—you have healers?" Luxen's hand dropped to Solo's chest, attempting to staunch the blood.

"Help!" Samiel cried out. He had the door open. "Help! Attack!"

He grinned at Solo's glance and prowled back across the room. He didn't want help, he was calling for angels to come, forcing Luxen to flee. But that was... good. Luxen couldn't be here.

Solo tore his gaze away from Samiel, fixing it instead on Luxen. "Go—you have to go. They'll kill you." A spasm of pain wracked him, his body fighting to cinch the wound. "They can't find you here."

"Solo, hush. If we stop the blood—"

"It's all right. I'll be all right." He shoved again. "Go, Lux. *Now*."

Luxen looked at the blood on his hands, then Samiel waiting by the balcony doors. He had to know there was no way he was leaving the chamber alive. "Tell them I did this. Don't defend me. I'm not worth it."

Solo would *never* condemn him like that. He shoved Luxen, putting force behind it, even some anger at the suggestion he'd lie, and fought from his arms. "Go!" He flared his wings, leaving no room for doubt. "Get out, now, before they—"

Angels tore through the doorway, into the room.

"C'mon, Lux!" Samiel yelled.

Luxen fled for the balcony. As long as he got away, everything would be all right. But the guards had seen. They surged across the room after him. Solo's heart stuttered.

"Wait—no, don't—" He staggered toward them but fell to a knee. Damn it! His body had failed him when he'd needed it the most.

Two angels launched from the balcony, but a third hung back, tending Solo. "General, you're hurt? Don't move. I'll summon healers."

After that there was just noise, shouts, thundering boots, and the swish of angel wings. He listened for word of Luxen and Samiel, but the healers who came knew nothing of their fates, and Solo could only send a silent prayer to Seraphim to save a more-than-worthy demon.

CHAPTER 16

*L*uxen

LUXEN PLUNGED FROM AERIE, through the clouds, chasing Samiel. Two angels hot on their wing-tips soon became four, and none of them showed any signs of slowing. There was nowhere to hide until they got among the streets of London. Samiel was ahead, wings thrown back and pinched together to alleviate drag. But Luxen gained, buzzing past him, his wings and body slimmer, an arrow through the air to Samiel's axe.

The cloud cover split open and Luxen swooped low over London's skyline. Gravity tried to yank out his insides. Blackness throbbed in his eyes. He fought it, pushing through. His wings burned, muscles near the breaking point. The bruises from his earlier fall blazed, threatening to weaken his wings. If that happened, nothing could save him from a hard landing against the side of an even harder building. He swooped, ducked, heart hammering and blood pumping fast through heated veins.

Samiel stayed in his slipstream, riding his wake. Few could outfly Luxen, as these angels would soon learn.

A glance over his shoulder revealed he'd lost one. They were down to three. But those three were as determined as any had been during the war. If they caught him, they'd kill him.

The old London Eye Ferris wheel, abandoned on the side of the Thames, emerged out of the gloom ahead. Time and war had bent and rusted its structure. Luxen tipped his wings, aiming for its mangled spokes. Let the angels try and follow him through there. At the last moment, he flared his wings, thrusting them out like sails to catch the wind, and beat them hard, flying vertical. Then he switched up again, tucking them in so he could plow through the warped metal. Something twanged behind him. Samiel snarled. Then an angel slammed into a steel girder. His howl echoed deep into London. Feathers flew.

Luxen dove low, sweeping again through buildings, then shot under a bridge. On the other side of the arch, a storm drain opened into the Thames. He banked in the air, dove into the drain opening, vanished his wings, and dropped to his feet, into a run. They'd lose them on the ground. It was the only way. Samiel lumbered behind, following him into the damp, stinking dark.

Rats squeaked. Filthy water sloshed around his ankles.

They climbed from the drain deep in the heart of abandoned warehouses. Luxen dashed into a barren building, and Samiel stumbled in behind him.

He dropped, hunkering down behind a low wall, and waited.

"Did we lose 'em?" Samiel panted, crouched behind him.

Luxen eyed the drain opening fewer than fifty paces away. Angels hated getting their feathers dirty. They were unlikely to follow them, but he also knew never to assume anything. Not when it came to angels.

"Luxen?"

"Quiet."

An angel climbed from the drain, his wings filthy. His snarl said he wasn't the sort to care.

Fuck.

"Let's get out of here," Samiel grumbled.

The angel looked over, fixing their hiding place in his sights. He'd heard Samiel. Their escape options were narrowing by the second.

Samiel peered over Luxen's shoulder. He grabbed his angelblade and growled, "It's just one. I can take him."

"No, leave him." Luxen shoved the heavier demon back. Windows gaped on the other side of the building. If they moved now, they might be able to slip away with no need for violence. "Let's go."

Samiel didn't move. "I'm fuckin' takin' him."

"Don't be an idiot. Leave him." Luxen grabbed his arm and tried to haul him back. "We'll lose him in the—"

Samiel's nostrils flared. "I don't take orders from you, Luxen. We kill them before they kill us. That's how it's always been. And that ain't changed because Lord Konstantin is fucking an angel!"

Samiel wasn't thinking. Killing an angel would cause more trouble than it was worth. But the rage in his eyes made it clear this wasn't war, this was personal. He wanted revenge, and while that angel bearing down on them wasn't Mikhail, any dead angel would suffice.

Luxen yanked on Samiel's arm, jerking him down. "Let it go. This won't change anything."

"You're the same as him." Samiel's top lip rippled over sharp teeth. *"Angelfucker."*

Samiel's heavy fist slammed Luxen facedown into the dirt before Luxen could see the swing coming. With his head spinning and his jaw burning from the punch, he managed to get his hands under him and lever himself upright. The ringing in his ears grew sharper; no, not ringing—swords clashing. Blood pooled under his tongue. He spat to the side and winced around the throbbing pain. Behind him, Samiel and the angel clashed viciously.

Samiel was bigger, stronger, but the angel was fast. Blood dribbled through Samiel's clothes. The angel had already landed his blade's edge, nicking Samiel's leathers.

He almost wished the angel would finish Samiel off. It would solve a lot of problems. But Samiel didn't deserve to die here. He had served Luxen faithfully. Luxen owed him.

Luxen scooped up a rock, gingerly climbed to his feet, and circled around, merging with the shadows. The angel was too preoccupied with Samiel to notice him. He waited for the right moment, for the angel's wings to lift—as they always did when angels skipped back—and Luxen lunged, cracking the rock over the back of the angel's head. The angel collapsed in a heap of filthy feathers.

Luxen kicked the angelblade away from his limp hand. Already moaning, he wasn't dead, and he wouldn't be down for long.

Samiel raised his blade in both hands, meaning to plunge it down through the angel's back.

Luxen darted in, wings spread. Samiel's blade shone. Samiel roared, brought it down—

The blade's tip hung poised over Luxen's chest.

Luxen swallowed. He hadn't been sure Samiel would stop. And he'd been strangely all right with his life ending here, if it must, defending an unknown fallen angel. He met the demon's gaze. "It's done. Leave it."

The growl that rumbled out of Samiel had Luxen's wings twitching, but the bigger demon lowered the blade. "It's not done until every angel pays."

This time when Luxen shoved him, Samiel finally backed up. Cut, bleeding, emotional, and exhausted, he was in no condition to go on. "It. Is. Done. Samiel."

Samiel threw Luxen a disgusted snarl but relented and turned away. "It's a long way from done, Luxen. You'd better decide whose side you're on, and fast. If you're turning into one of *them*, you're dead to me."

Samiel clambered over fallen bricks, and Luxen had no choice but to follow. Where else could he go?

He glanced down at the unconscious angel. There had been a time he'd have killed him. The only good angel was a dead angel. But this vulnerable male, his feathers wet, glued together with filth, he wasn't a threat. Where for so long there had been hatred for angels, now he just felt tired.

CHAPTER 17

Solo

Solo laced up his over-jacket—back in flight leathers after two weeks' rehabilitation. The healers had told him not to do any aerobatic flying in case the wound in his chest reopened, but he had to get out of the hospital room and stretch his wings before he lost his damned mind.

And he missed the cats. Severn had been feeding them, but Severn wasn't Solo. They needed him. Or maybe he needed them. He didn't think too much about that and instead thanked the healers and climbed onto the hospital's rooftop to stand in the sun. He gave his wings a few experimental flaps to shake off their stiffness. Some of the feathers were bent and dusty. A blast through the sky would take care of those.

He hopped off the roof, spread his wings, and soared over London's winding streets. Humans bustled below.

Their lives were always so busy. Sunlight baked his wings, warming them through, and by the time he reached his house, he began to feel much like his normal self again.

Vanishing his wings, he opened the door, almost tripped over a mewing Two, and bent to stroke his fur and tickle his chin.

"Oh, thank Aerius you're back," Severn grumbled from the kitchen at the back of the house. "Your cats are a menace." There were *many* cats in the kitchen, all snaking around Severn's legs. "One threw up on the stairs." Severn handed him a sachet of food. "Here, they can rub against you now. I have fluff where no demon should have fluff." He sounded strung out, but his smile was kind. "It's good to have you back."

"I'm happy to be back."

Severn leaned against the countertop. "You think you're up for duty?"

"I feel fine."

"Yeah, but... What about the rest of you? Luxen did a number on you."

"Like I said, I'm fine." Solo busied himself opening the sachet of food and squishing its contents into a bowl, only to be rushed by multiple furry bodies and flicking tails. He tossed the empty sachet in the trash and looked for something else to occupy himself so he didn't have to meet Severn's gaze. They all thought he'd been brainwashed by Luxen, culminating in Luxen's attack in his chambers. Nothing could be further from the truth, but he knew better than to tell them that. They'd keep him off duty forever unless he told them what they wanted to hear. And he needed to get back out there to find Luxen. To make this right. "So... how are things?"

"If you're asking whether we've found Samiel and Luxen? No. They've gone to ground. It's unlikely we'll find either of them anytime soon. If they're smart, they'll have already left London."

"Yes. That would be good," he replied automatically.

Tell them it was me.

Solo huffed a breath, trying to keep his breathing steady. It was wrong. The way they'd treated Luxen, the way they continued to treat him, chasing him down like he was vermin.

Luxen wasn't bad. He was *complicated*. But so was Severn, so was Mikhail. How was Luxen so different to them? They had all done terrible things in the war, and they'd all learned and changed and grown. So had Luxen. Solo knew, because of those last words: *Tell them it was me.* Luxen had been trying to protect Solo. In human stories, the villain did not protect the hero. Luxen wasn't the villain and Solo was going to prove it.

"Solo?"

"Huh?"

"I asked if there were any lingering effects—" Severn's brow pinched. "—mentally?"

"No." Solo swallowed. "I just..." With the cats fed and happy, he leaned against the opposite counter, and remembered how Luxen had stood where Severn was now, and how he'd surrendered his sandwiches to the cats. Solo sighed. "When you and Mikhail... Well, when you knew you were supposed to be together, what did it feel like?"

Severn grabbed a chair from the nearby set and managed to squeeze his demon ass into it. "Are you asking me what love feels like?"

"I think so. Yes. How do you know it's love?"

Severn breathed in, filling his lungs. His broad chest expanded, and if he'd had his wings out they would have stretched. He leaned an arm on the little table and cast his gaze about the kitchen. Whatever he saw was far away, or deep inside. Memories, perhaps. "Angels called love the allyanse because they couldn't explain why one emotion should change everything in their lives. But it does. Like you've carved out half your heart and handed it to someone."

Solo winced. "Sounds painful."

"Oh, it is." Severn chuckled. "But when they take that piece of your heart, it's as though before you were incomplete, but now you're whole."

That made sense. That feeling of completeness. Solo understood that. "But what if you just like someone?"

"That's okay too. Love is what you make it. It doesn't have to be defined and it's not the same for everyone. The love you have for your horde of cats is different to the love you might find with another angel or demon."

He understood that too, but he still didn't understand how you knew it was definitely love and not just... the fucking. "Is there... a test? A way to know if you're in love?"

"Sure." Severn grinned. "But it's different for everyone." He rose from the chair and rested a hand on Solo's shoulder. "You'll know it when it happens."

"What if it doesn't happen? Or what if it happens and I miss it? What if it's already happened and I let it go?"

"Solo..." Severn sighed. "If it's meant to be, it will happen and you won't miss it, trust me. You'll know because the person you love, whoever that person will be, you'll protect them, defend them, save them. Do anything and everything for them. Because they have a half of your heart. There were times I wanted to kill Mikhail—honestly, there still are—but I'd raze London for him. I'd fight every demon and angel for him."

Their love was a wonder. Solo smiled. "You already did."

"Yeah... I kinda did." He patted Solo's shoulder. "You got this. Come back to Aerie when you're ready. We could do with your brains up there. Too many of our kind fear change. We need your reason and clarity among us."

He nodded. "I'll be there."

Severn left. Solo made sure the cats were content. He dealt with the mess on the stairs, climbed to the attic and out, onto the roof, then sat with his legs dangling over the edge and his wings basking behind him. The city hummed. Angels flew overhead, their feathers occasionally catching the sunlight, making them sparkle like daytime stars.

I was afraid of stars.
Tell them I did this.

It hadn't been a lie. Or concubi allure.

Luxen had protected Solo.

You'll protect them, defend them, save them, Severn had said.

Did Luxen care for Solo? Why else would he have said those things. He'd cared enough to make all of Aerie think he'd attacked Solo, and Solo had done nothing to protect Luxen in return. He'd tried to defend him to Mikhail, but nobody had listened. It wasn't enough. Solo wanted to do more. Wanted to find him and show everyone that if they were entitled to change, then so was Luxen.

And maybe, above all of that, he missed Luxen. His warmth, his wings, his crooked smile, and his deep, rumbling laugh. He missed the way his eyes widened whenever Solo spread his feathers, or the way he'd cradle Solo's head in his big hand. He missed his body, and how firm and powerful Luxen had felt, rocking beneath him. How *powerful* it had made Solo feel to be permitted to touch and stroke and pull him close.

If loving someone was handing them half your heart, he thought maybe Luxen had somehow taken half of his and without it, without Luxen, some part of Solo was missing.

There was only one thing to do.

Find Luxen and ask if he felt it too.

CHAPTER 18

Luxen

Two weeks since Luxen had escaped the enclosure.

Two weeks since he'd lain with the angel, Solomon.

Two weeks of torture.

Dagenham's demon bars were rowdy, noisy, the air full of ether, from lust or pride or anger; pick an emotion—it was everywhere, reaching for him, creeping over his skin. But none of it sated the bone-aching need within.

This place, packed wall-to-wall with demons, would have fed him for days before. He'd have summoned two or three of his kin, clicked his fingers, and they'd have gone down on him, pleasured him for hours. He'd have taken them in every way, fucked their every hole and relished it. He was a concubi lord; he'd have bathed in emotional ether and been worshipped for it.

Now, he was reduced to sulking in the shadowy corner

of the bar, in the hope no angels came in and recognized him. He didn't think the demons here would give him up to Mikhail's forces. Luxen still had allies. But angels had been known to visit, to see how demons relaxed, to get down and roll in the dirt with demons.

He should feed, but he had no interest in it.

"Hey." Samiel leaned an arm on the bar.

No, *my Lord*. No bow of the head. Just hey. How far Luxen had fallen.

"You look like a beaten dog."

"Hm." Luxen threw back the last of his whiskey. The seventh glass he'd had in an hour. "What do you want, Samiel?"

"They're meeting. Tonight. You should be there."

The last time he and Samiel had met, Samiel had spoken of a resistance cell, a group of demons who wanted a return to the old way of things, but Luxen had dismissed the claims as barely worth his time. And he'd been distracted by this wretched hole in his heart. "Why?"

"They *want* you there." Samiel snorted. "They don't trust Konstantin now he spends all his time in angelcity. They want a proper demon lord. I didn't tell them how I found you soft for angel. Help them—*us*—and maybe I'll forget what I saw?" His eyes twinkled with knowing.

Luxen raised a hand and had the demon behind the bar refill his glass. A nice piece of ass, that one. A bit young. But strong. He had his wings hidden. They all did, to save space, but Luxen figured the male's would be broad. He'd caught Luxen's less than subtle glances earlier in the evening. He'd be game. Most demons were. Luxen had never had trouble picking who he'd wanted to fuck. The trouble now, it seemed, was that none of them had scarlet feathers and auburn freckles.

He chuckled at his own insanity. Konstantin had warned him that once he'd had angel, nothing would compare. The bastard was right.

The bartender picked up a tall, thin glass and wiped it down with a damp cloth. His amber eyes skipped to Luxen, and his wiping motions turned suggestive.

"Well?" Samiel asked.

"Well, what?" Luxen drawled, torn between Samiel's glower and the bartender's pumping motions.

"Are you coming?"

"That's what I'd like to know." The bartender smirked.

"Fine." If it was the only way to get Samiel off his back. "I'll be right there."

"Don't keep me waiting." Samiel left his side, disappearing into the crowd.

The bartender planted his elbows on the bar and propped his chin in his hand. His two, tightly coiled horns protruded from a mop of bronze hair. "I won't be missed..." he said, alluding to how Luxen might want to take up the proposition *to come.*

A quick fuck out back might alleviate the hollowness he was feeling, top him up on ether, but even as he considered it, he was saying, "Another time." As though someone else had control of him.

"Your loss." He straightened, dropped a shoulder, and smirked.

"No doubt."

What was wrong with him? When had a concubi ever declined sex? He needed to fuck, and he needed to feed. These were fundamental. He could not live without them.

What did he think was going to happen? That Solomon was going to appear in a demon bar, suck him off in some dingy corridor, then fly back to Aerie, to his life, and all would be well?

Luxen downed the eighth glass, snarled at his self-depreciating idiocy, and fought through the crowd to escape the bar.

Outside, Samiel sat perched on a bench, his feet on the slats and his ass on the back, wings catching the streetlights.

"That was quick."

"Doesn't take long," Luxen said, adding a salacious smile in the hope it stopped any further questions. "Show me what this resistance is made of."

They walked south, down a few winding alleys, coming to a door in a building with bricked-up windows. Samiel knocked, and when the small viewing hatch opened, he grunted at the person inside. Apparently, that was all it took for them to open the door.

Stairs led down into an old basement, probably used for storage. It was dry, warm, and secure, and full of demons. The voices hushed, like waves receding from a beach, and in near silence Luxen descended the last few steps. While he wasn't heavier than any of them here, he was taller and was able to meet each and every demon's gaze.

"Lord Luxen," a stout demon with green-tinted skin grumbled. "You were taken to Aerie?"

"I was. But, as you can see, I'm fine."

"We can't trust those angels—" another voice murmured.

"They'll stab us in the back like they stab their own."

Dissent rippled through them, growing, like flames on kindling. It wasn't long before they were all voicing fears and anger and unknowns. All concerns they had a right to air. Luxen heard them all, understood them. Like him, they'd been raised on bloodshed and battle. They knew little else.

Samiel's eyebrow arched. "Well?"

Luxen raised his hands and began to drift among them. "Demons... Hush now." They parted for him, making way. "I share in your concerns. Trust is earned, not freely given. Konstantin is High Lord, but what does he truly know of our plight when he's spent the last ten years among the enemy, living as one of them?"

Jeers and agreement simmered.

"Tell me your plan," Luxen said. "You must have one. Or did you just gather here to bitch like pups?"

"We have a plan," a familiar gravelly yet somehow smooth female tone rose.

The path through the crowd had led him to a table, where the demon sat on its edge, one leg bent. Luxen narrowed his eyes on Djall, Konstantin's sister.

"But first we need to know," Djall added, "are you in?"

CHAPTER 19

Solo

MIKHAIL HAD GATHERED the demon lords and higher angels together—the new council—as they were called, to discuss a troubling development. Solo had been busy organizing patrols, as Aerie continued to be locked down. He'd been summoned at the last moment and rushed to the chamber still in his battle leathers.

Severn was here, looking grim. But Djall was absent. He hadn't seen much of her lately. If there was trouble, she was usually the first to find it.

In fact, all the faces were severe. The arrival of the European Guardian Angel was in two days, but instead of presenting a cool, calm united front, Aerie was close to chaos. Peace between demon and angel teetered on a blade's edge.

Mikhail went through the formalities of greeting them

all, including the demons and their great Manors—the families they came from. "Luxen has resurfaced."

Solo caught his mind wandering and whipped it back into the moment, then tried to slow his leaping heart and stop his wings from twitching and giving his sudden interest away. He'd made his own enquiries into Luxen's whereabouts, even asking the young pup, Ernas, to keep an eye on the streets, but as far as anyone knew, Luxen had gone to ground.

"But I'm afraid it's as we feared. He commands a small but influential cell of individuals who desire a return to war."

Solo steeled himself to keep from blurting out demands for proof. Mikhail would get to that. He glimpsed Severn watching him then slid his gaze back to Mikhail while his heartbeat hammered in his ears. He did not believe for a single second that Luxen *wanted* war. He hated most angels, and he had good reasons to. During the war, he'd issued orders to fight and kill angels but he'd done so in the name of protecting demons.

Actively seeking war again?

No. Luxen wasn't foolish. He didn't want to see more dead.

Samiel though? Solo knew so little about him... But he'd been in his chamber with Luxen, he'd had some kind of influence over him. Samiel, Solo did not trust.

"Solo?"

"Yes, Your Grace?"

"Do you have anything to say?"

He cleared his throat and pulled his fanned wings in, not having realized he'd opened them, making everyone peer at him. "What proof do you have of Luxen's involvement?"

"Proof?" Severn grumbled beside Mikhail. "Proof he's a manipulative snake or proof he wants Mikhail dead?"

Of course Severn would leap straight to the worst possible explanation. "Forgive me, and I mean no disrespect when I say this, but could it be your emotions are clouding your judgment?"

Severn blinked. "What?"

The temperature in the chambers plummeted. "Proof then? What proof do you have of Luxen's involvement in this group? Did you see him?"

"No." Severn growled.

"So we're to condemn him on gossip?"

"No." Severn unfolded his arms. "We have a reliable witness."

"Is this the same witness who saw Luxen with an angelblade, who claims he killed the guard? Because I put in a request to question that witness but it seems they've conveniently disappeared."

Severn wet his lips slowly. "Be careful with your words, Solo. You're beginning to sound as though you're accusing me of something."

"No, that's not... That is not my intention." Oh dear. Most everyone around the table was scowling at him. He needed to walk this back. "I just feel that there are a great many people who dislike the ex-High Lord who might be inclined to fabricate so-called truths in an effort to alienate him."

"Nobody needs to fabricate anything. The prick alienated himself—"

Mikhail put his hand out. He and Severn shared a look and Severn's fire cooled.

"The witness in this case is undisputable," Mikhail said. "You have good instincts, Solomon. But in this, Luxen is indefensible."

There was a time Solo would have let it rest there. Mikhail's word was law. But Mikhail himself had freed Solo from the binds of dutiful loyalty. He did not have to stand back and blindly follow Mikhail's orders. Too much had changed for that. "Your Grace, may I speak with you privately?" Mikhail owed him that much.

"Very well."

They left Severn at the head of the table and Mikhail led Solo into a comfortable side-chamber with a vacant desk used for occasional meetings and a balcony, its doors closed to the wind.

"Before you begin," Mikhail said. "It has only been a few weeks since Luxen assaulted you—"

"He did not assault me, Your Grace. And he did not use his allure—although nobody appears to believe me in either instances. Do I appear so weak to you that I'd let a demon seduce me with lies, work his way into my chamber, to get to you? Do you think so little of me, Mikhail?" He could feel his rage rising and had to temper it back. But he wasn't the only one struggling. Mikhail had gone very still in front of the desk.

"There is no weakness in being his victim."

"I wasn't—" Solo stopped himself and swallowed the rest, knowing how Luxen *had* manipulated Mikhail. Or tried to. Had almost succeeded. "He was different then... with you."

"You're telling me Luxen has changed in the space of a few weeks?"

It did sound ludicrous. But it had happened before. "Why not? You did."

"Solo... He used you to get out of the enclosure, and then he used you to get inside Aerie—"

Solo sighed. "That wasn't what happened. Why won't you believe me?"

"Because Luxen right now plots against us, against me, against this peace. And I cannot have him bring down everything we've worked for. I won't allow it. He must be stopped. By any means."

Solo sighed. "Let me go to him—"

"No."

"Your Grace—Mikhail?"

"No. He almost killed you."

"That wasn't..." Solo chuckled; it was that or scream. "You know, you can't change alone. I used to think it was possible, and maybe it is for some angels and demons, but we need each other. You had Severn, and together you changed. I saw it—Severn changed physically, but that's not what I mean. You saved each other. Luxen *wants* to change, but everyone keeps putting him back in the same box he was in before. He only knows how to manipulate his way out of the corner he keeps getting backed into. You won't believe me and nobody will believe him, so what choice does he have? He told me to tell you he stabbed me because he knew it would make things easier *for me*. But I won't lie to condemn him."

"Would you lie to save him?"

Solo already had. Or tried to. He looked away, and Mikhail had his answer.

"He's in your head," Mikhail said softly. "I can't trust you."

"No, he's in *your* head. The old him. And I'm sorry for that. You and Severn won't hear me out. You'll condemn him, like everyone condemned you. And the fact you can't or won't see that makes you a hypocrite."

Mikhail lifted his chin. His wings clamped together. "I appreciate your honesty but it's clear having you back so soon was a mistake. We won't be needing your service for the foreseeable future. You may leave Aerie."

"That's how it's going to be?" Solo smiled and backed toward the balcony doors. "If we begin this peace with the killing of a demon who wants to change, then maybe we don't deserve peace at all."

Solo pushed the balcony doors open and dove from the balcony's edge, into the air. He had to find Luxen before Severn and Mikhail did. In this, they hadn't changed. They would hunt and kill him. They had all of Aerie with them; most demons and angels were on their side. Luxen was alone.

No, not alone. He had someone.

He had Solo.

He just didn't know it yet.

CHAPTER 20

*S*olo

Two days had passed since Solo had walked out on Mikhail. Today was the day of the Guardian's visit. The skies outside were grey and laden with rain that hadn't yet begun to fall. With no wind to stir the air, it was as though all of London held its breath, *waiting*.

He'd had no luck sending Ernas out to search for Luxen and had been about to resort to walking the demon streets himself—not as dangerous a prospect as it would have been before peace, but still risky—when a knock sounded on his front door.

Ernas, the blue-skinned wily demon, stood on his doorstep. He grinned and dropped his hood. His previously stumpy horns had begun to grow in, and where he'd been scrawny before, muscle was filling him out. "I found him." His smile fell. "But you ain't gonna like it."

"Take me there."

"Er..." Ernas gave Solo the visual once-over. "Okay, but not like that." He gestured at Solo's clothes—lightweight, loose-fitting linens. "You got jeans and a coat, or something... less angel?"

Solo peered down at himself. He had his leathers and could throw on a hooded jacket. After hurrying back inside, he quickly changed.

"Don't bring a blade!" Ernas called from the step. "You don't wanna be found in demon town with a blade," he added when Solo returned.

"Better?" Solo asked.

Ernas's face screwed up. He squinted, assessing the tightly fitting demon leathers. "Yeah, I guess. But now you look like an angel trying to be a demon."

"There's not much I can do about that." Solo left the house and descended the steps to street level. "I thought angels were welcome in er... demon town—Dagenham?"

"Sure they are." Ernas grinned in a way that suggested an angel's welcome might be different to a demon one. He flicked out his wings. "You all right to fly in this?" He gestured upward with a thumb.

The threat of rain was close, but the air was dry. "Yes." Solo revealed his own wings, shivering some as the cool air stroked over his feathers. "As long as it stays dry."

"All those fancy feathers and you can't get 'em wet." Ernas chuckled, then lifted off with a blast of leathery wings. "Let's go, angel."

Solo carved through the air after the young pup's silhouette. Ernas had helped him during those fretful final hours in which Luxen and Samiel had tried to kill Severn and Mikhail. He'd learned later that the demon god,

Aerius, had been the demon who had caught Solo—saved him, taken him back to their den where he'd met Ernas. Aerius had saved Ernas too. Solo didn't fully understand his own part on everything that had happened, just that Aerius had intervened when they'd been needed the most, and Solo was grateful for that. He'd never forget falling from Aerie, his wings bound... knowing, without any doubt, that his time in this world had been about to be over.

In battle, he'd stared death in the eyes a hundred times, but never like that... Falling from Aerie had been the only time he'd been afraid to die.

Ernas pointed down among tightly packed houses and crooked streets. Solo spiraled downward and landed on a rooftop after him.

"Hide the wings," Ernas said, hands tucked in his pockets. "Put your hood up."

Solo did both.

"Can you do anything about your face?" He waved a hand at his face.

"What's wrong with my face?"

"Just... I dunno... You're super pretty, is all."

"Oh. Er. No. Not really."

Ernas harrumphed and ruffled his wings. "Just don't be too angel-like, okay?"

"Erm... okay." He wasn't sure how not to be an angel, but he'd give it a shot.

They took a stairwell zigzagging down the outside of the building, down to street level, and began walking the street among demons. Solo had heard of the cauldron. A place beneath Aerie where half-demons, cambion, had tried to make a home for themselves. Much of it had been destroyed when Aerie's original disks fell, but this place had the same ramshackle ambience, with drum fires, pop-up market stalls, and a strong sense that everyone knew everyone else. And nobody knew Solo. Gazes raked over him. Slimmer than a demon, it was obvious at a glance that he was angel, but there were other angels here. Even an angel who had his wings out and appeared to be smoking something, passing the cigarette to the demon next to him.

Solo yanked his gaze away. Then discreetly glanced back again. The demon handed the cigarette back, and the angel took it, brought it to his lips—

"Here." Ernas pushed through a door of an old brick-fronted building, releasing a blast of music and chatter from inside. A bar. Solo bumped into someone, mumbled an apology, and got a grunt in reply. Someone else nudged him in the side. Ernas grabbed Solo's arm and hauled him through the fray to the bar.

Everyone inside was so *big*. Horns scraped the ceiling. Muscles bulged from tight shirts. Demons were packed into the bar from wall to wall. They all had their wings hidden or nobody would be able to move.

"What can I get you both?" a demon behind the bar asked. His gaze skimmed Ernas, then darted to Solo and his golden eyes narrowed, but he didn't say the obvious. *Oh, you're an angel.*

"Just two beers," Ernas said, and when the bartender left to fix the beers, he turned to Solo. "I'm going to see if he's around. Sit here. Don't talk to anyone. Don't make eye contact with anyone and you'll be fine."

He wished he'd brought a blade.

The bartender brought their bottled beers and Ernas

smirked into his. Why did Solo get the impression the young demon was enjoying this a lot more than he should have been.

"It's all right, angel," he said, catching Solo's glower. "Nobody here will hurt you. Too many witnesses." He laughed to himself then slunk off into the crowd to go look for Luxen, leaving Solo alone.

Solo picked at the beer's label. He'd only ever been surrounded by this many demons in battle. It seemed strange not to be wielding a blade. They probably thought the same about having an angel among them.

The bartender gave him sideways glances.

Solo sipped his beer, not disliking the taste but not enjoying it either. Severn had told him once how he'd tried to get Mikhail drunk on wine—apparently, it took a lot to get an angel intoxicated.

The bartender drifted over. "Your friend left?" He had an easy smile and nice eyes. His horns were a bit small, compared to Luxen's, but like most demons, he carried ample muscle in his shoulders and arms, with a thick waist too.

"He's coming back."

"Uh huh. You should be careful. Angel like you in a place like this..."

"Thank you for the concern, but I can handle myself."

The demon leaned on the bar. "Yeah?" His gaze began to wander. "We get some of you in here. Curious types. Not many as pretty as you, though. If you want, I can find you a demon piece of ass to take a ride on?"

Solo blinked. "What?"

"That's what you're here for, right? Sample the double D?"

"Er—"

"Demon dick? You look like demon bait. All uptight and reserved until you get between the sheets, eh?"

Wait, he could tell that by looking at Solo? "What makes you say that?" he asked. He *was* curious. The demon was right about that. And maybe... he was right about the between the sheets part too. Solo did feel tight and reserved, but when he'd been with Luxen, all of that had fallen away, leaving him loose and free.

"You're strong, I can tell. Although, you don't look it. It's in your eyes. You can see an angel's heart through his eyes."

By Seraphim. "You can?"

"Sure." The bartender reached out and touched Solo's cheek. "Yours just might be the prettiest green eyes I've ever seen."

Solo caught his wrist and twisted, jerking the demon against the bar. He wasn't sure why he'd stopped him, just that the touching was a step too far for someone he didn't know.

"Gah! Hey—"

"Hey, angel, get your hands off him," a deep thunderous voice growled from the crowd.

Solo shoved the bartender back, letting him go, and regarded the big brute of a demon looming to his left. "We were just having a conversation. That conversation is over now."

"You don't touch a demon in 'ere without his permission, you get me?" the demon said with a growl.

"I didn't." The back of Solo's neck prickled. Other demons had turned toward them. Solo was already in a corner. And now he was peering at four of them moving in to encircle him. Slowly, he climbed from the barstool and straightened. "He touched me."

The big demon glanced at the bartender, who shrugged, rubbing his wrist.

"You should leave."

"I'm waiting for my friend." Solo lowered his hood. If they were going to attack, he needed to see his peripheral vision.

"So wait outside." The big demon sneered.

"He told me to wait here, so I'm going to wait here." Solo's wings itched to spring free but he kept them illusioned away. His fingers twitched to grab an angelblade he didn't have. He wasn't going to be bullied from a bar when he'd done nothing wrong.

The demon's big hand reached out. Quick as a whip, Solo caught his arm, danced sideways, bent his thick arm backward, and shoved him face-first against the wall. He leaned into the demon, pinning him. He barked a cry, more from surprise than pain.

Solo glanced behind him. The others were moving in. "Stay back or I break his arm." To prove he could, he bent the demon's arm at an angle it didn't want to go, making the demon growl.

"Fellas!" Ernas slipped between them, hands up, and laughed. "C'mon... what's going on here? Eh? You let one angel get you all hot and bothered? What'd he do, spill your drinks? C'mon... easy. Eh? What's he gonna do? There are like, sixty of you and one of him. Don't be dicks about this." Ernas caught Solo's eye. "Time to go, *angel*."

Solo freed the demon but held the brute's glare as he righted his clothes and sneered at Solo. He might want to get a swing in to prove he could. Solo guarded for it. But the brute backed off and the crowd absorbed the group again.

Ernas rolled his eyes and landed a hand on Solo's shoulder, guiding him through the crowd. "I leave you alone for five minutes and you start a fight?"

"I didn't start anything. The bartender got handsy—"

"Oh yeah, he does that. I should have warned you. Anyway… c'mon. I found him, but… Listen—" He tilted his head close. "—you're not gonna like it."

"So what's new?" Solo tugged his sleeves and smoothed his hair, trying to compose himself. "I haven't liked any of this so far."

"Yeah, okay, but… You sure you want to see him now?"

"Yes. Don't delay. I have to see him." His pulse quickened. Just the thought of seeing Luxen again was enough to make his blood rush. Strange, that a demon he'd only recently come to know should have such a physical effect on him. Wonderful, but strange. He had to warn him how Mikhail and Severn were coming for him, how they had a witness, someone on the inside. Nothing else mattered.

"All right." Ernas opened a side door, revealing a long, dingy corridor. "Let's go."

CHAPTER 21

*L*uxen

HE'D HAVE PREFERRED it if the three males writhing on the bed were all angels. The ether hit he got from angels far outweighed that of demons. But one angel and two demons was enough to top him up, and he rather enjoyed the contrast of angel and demon skin sliding together under soft candlelight.

He reclined in the wingback chair, watching the angel get fucked from behind, while the angel sucked demon dick. Jealousy spiked inside him—jealous of those demons, touching angel skin, especially the one behind, gripping the angel's sweat-soaked wings. Luxen had lost count of the times he'd fantasized the same. Although, the imaginary angel from his dreams had become one of red feathers and red hair scrunched in Luxen's fists.

The longer he spent with his own kind, the more

dreamlike his time with Solo became. An angel like Solo couldn't want a demon like Luxen. It had to be a dream because good things like Solo did not fall into Luxen's lap. Ever.

He'd dreamed he could be different too. As though, maybe, he might not be the villain in someone's story. He'd hoped, just once, that he might be a hero. But those thoughts were foolish fantasies. Fantasies he wouldn't have even bothered to entertain until meeting Solo. That angel was a bad influence on him.

He scooped up the whiskey glass and sipped while his body absorbed the excess ether rippling off the threesome.

There was a time he'd have been among them. He wasn't sure why he wasn't. A great many things didn't make any sense. Like the feeling of guilt and shame he got every time he met with the rebels to plan Konstantin's downfall. He despised the High Lord. Konstantin was everything that was wrong in this world. He should die. Or so Luxen kept telling himself. But he suspected, too, that things had become more complicated of late. As though, perhaps, he might be wrong about Konstantin.

The three were reaching their crescendo, skin slapping on skin, wings shuddering, feathers gleaming in candlelight. It was beautiful. Demon and angel entwined. And that thought was proof Luxen had clearly gone insane.

A knock sounded on the door.

Ether spluttered. The threesome faltered, their rising ecstasy stuttering as their minds switched from being lost in each other to wondering who had dared interrupt them.

Luxen rose from the chair. He waved at the three to continue. Whoever had dared interrupt him was about to learn not to fuck with a feeding concubi.

He reached for the handle. The door flung open, and a hooded angel rushed into the room, then tripped to an awkward halt.

The scent of meadows and sunshine barreled into Luxen, knocking him back a step.

The angel, Solo—it couldn't be anyone else—dropped his hood. He stared at the threesome, his russet eyebrows pinching together. After absorbing the sight of them fucking, he peered at Luxen.

Ernas shrank behind Solo. "Er... Luxen. Let me explain. He was looking—"

"Get out," Luxen snarled at the pup.

"What is this?" Solo asked, but it wasn't curiosity driving the question. His eyes burned with anger.

"This is... my life," Luxen heard himself explain, fearing it would turn Solo away for good, and maybe that should happen because the angel had no business being here.

Solo's face darkened some more. The candlelight wasn't soft on him. If anything, it had sharpened all his edges.

An unbidden growl rumbled through Luxen. "Get out. All of you." Nobody moved. "Now!"

"No." Solo folded his arms. "No. Carry on. Pretend I'm not here."

Ernas backed up. "I'm just gonna... go."

Luxen barely registered the pup leaving. He only had eyes for Solo, and Solo was staring at the three on the bed, still engaged with each other but sharing anxious glances.

Anger simmered off Solo like a heat-haze, already a hundred times more potent than the ether rising off the threesome. Luxen needed that. He'd been aching for that ether since leaving Solo's bed. Searching for it. Needing it.

And here he was, having barged right in on a scene any angel would be shocked by.

"I said continue," Solo growled. He popped himself against the far wall, arms crossed, and arched an eyebrow at Luxen in a sassy look that spilled lust through every single one of Luxen's veins, setting him ablaze. Fuck. He hadn't been hard during this session... until now.

"You heard him." Luxen retreated to his chair and lowered himself into it, heart pumping, skin prickling, dick becoming a hard rod trapped in his trousers.

The three didn't need any more encouragement and within minutes, they were squeezing, sliding, mouthing, kissing, pinching, biting, and fucking all over again. Luxen sipped his whiskey. He didn't need to watch them; he didn't want to—he watched only Solo. Watched how a bulge grew in the crotch of his trousers, how his eyes blazed bottle-green, and how fury and lust mingled within his ether, intoxicating Luxen as it filled the air. What was he angry at? Luxen, for being here? Himself, for liking this? The world?

So much anger, so much lust. He was building, ready to blow. Luxen salivated at the thought of being the one to light that dynamite.

The demon pounding into the angel's ass had the angel's wings bent backward, his cock buried deep, and from his ether alone, Luxen knew he was close to coming. Luxen's own cock pulsed, but not from wanting what the demon had—from watching how Solo's eyes dilated, how his lips parted, and the tip of his tongue slipped over them, and how he reached down to adjust his trousers hugging his dick.

Did he want to be among them?

Would he let them fuck him?

Did he want to fuck them?

So many possibilities.

Unable to stand it any longer, Luxen set his glass down, got to his feet, and approached Solo carefully, like approaching a wild animal, unsure if it was about to lash out or bolt. Solo didn't take his eyes off the threesome as Luxen stopped close against his shoulder. Luxen wanted to touch him, to sweep his hair back from his neck and kiss him there, to take him in his hands, shove him against the wall, and make him feel how Luxen blazed for him. But he did none of that. "Do you want that?" he whispered, gaze on Solo's face.

"No," Solo said, his voice thin. A lie.

Luxen fought the smile from his lips. Behind him, he heard the demon's panted breaths stuttering, his body about to unload deep inside the angel. Luxen might have given his right wing to be that demon behind Solo, if he wanted it.

The angel getting fucked moaned around the second demon's cock, and the male pounding his ass finally came, slapping hard, growling and shuddering. Solo's green eyes widened. His dark pupils swelled, drinking in the scene behind Luxen.

Luxen braced an arm against the wall and slid his free hand down Solo's chest, all the way down, stopping to cup his hard cock through his trousers. Solo let out a gasp and then swallowed hard.

"Do you want me like that?" Luxen whispered. "Tell me, Solo, what you want. I'll make it happen." He'd make *anything* happen. All Solo had to do was ask.

Solo's shining eyes skipped to Luxen's face. "Yes."

Fuck. Luxen might come from the word alone. *Yes*, from his angel. *Yes*. Had there ever been a finer word? Luxen removed his hand from the wall and slid it down Solo's back, drawing Solo to him. His own cock he pushed against Solo's hip, leaving the angel no doubt that it was him Luxen wanted.

"Tell me how," Luxen purred.

Solo's eyes narrowed. "What if it's wrong?"

"Nothing you can want is wrong."

Solo sighed, as though those words unshackled him. "Get on the bed. With them."

Luxen swallowed, his throat constricting. Nobody had ever dared tell him what to do during sex. But to hear Solo demand things of him, it ignited a delicious thrill inside him. He faced the trio, ushered the spent demon aside, and climbed onto the bed, on his knees.

"Show me your wings," Solo said.

The words had barely left his lips before Luxen freed his wings, rolling his shoulders to work out any stiffness. The angel had stopped sucking off the demon and watched over his shoulder as Solo ordered Luxen, his face curious. The demon, too, remained quiet and observant, waiting.

Solo walked to the end of the bed and stepped backed, studying the scene. He made no attempt to hide his protruding dick. Luxen's mouth watered at the many ideas spilling into his head.

"Kiss the angel," Solo said.

Luxen drew the angel up and kissed him, tasting demon saltiness and not caring. The angel moaned and dropped his hand.

"No, you don't touch him," Solo warned, adding his own throaty growl. "Only I touch Luxen."

Luxen's wings shuddered. His cock leaked, so erect he might come had the angel gotten his hand on it. He wanted Solo in his arms, Solo to kiss, to fuck... And the sly look in Solo's eyes said he knew it.

"Take the angel's member—his cock—in your mouth and make him come." Color flushed Solo's face and behind him, his wings shivered into sight, each red feather lit up like fire. The words were new to him. All of this was new to him, but he was *loving* it.

Luxen bent low, swallowed angel cock, heard Solo warn about touching again, and then wrapped his tongue and hand around the angel's dick. Not Solo's dick. That was what he really wanted between his lips. Solo knew that too. He had a wicked streak, and Luxen just might die for it.

The angel came readily, spilling salty seed over Luxen's tongue. He swallowed it fast and lifted off, licking his lips, to find Solo with his wings spread and his chest heaving. How much restraint did he have? When he blew, he might wash half of London in ether.

"I er... I came too," the demon admitted. "I had to."

Luxen smirked and nodded at Solo. "You've spent these two. Are you ready to take me, angel?"

"Out. Everyone."

The satisfied trio collected their clothes and hurried from the room. Luxen—on his knees on the bed, cock a burning rod, wings spread—waited.

The door clicked closed and Solo lifted his scorching gaze. "Take your cock out."

Luxen unlaced his trousers and got his dick in hand, freeing it from the tightness, but now he had his hand on his slick length and Solo's gaze on it, too, and all it would take was a few pumps and he wouldn't be able to hold back. He'd rarely been so jacked.

Solo's mouth ticked up at one corner. He pulled his hooded jacket off but thought better about removing his shirt. And instead of unlacing his trousers, he approached the bed. "Free me."

Luxen shuffled forward on his knees and made quick work of Solo's trouser ties. "You like giving orders."

"I do." Solo brushed his hand away. "I like making you desperate for the fuck."

A mangled moan slipped from Luxen. "You have a dark streak, angel. It's killing me." He panted hard. Solo was within grabbing distance. He could haul him into a kiss, make him moan and scream and come. But Solo was in charge.

"Hm..." Solo wrapped his fingers around Luxen's dick and flicked his tongue over Luxen's mouth. "I'm learning what I like."

"Do you like me?"

"I do."

Luxen chased his mouth, seeking the kiss that Solo kept from him. "Do you like *us*?"

"I do." He caught Luxen's jaw, holding him still. "I want your cock in me from behind, like that demon did with that angel. I want you to hold my wings and fuck me deep until you come. And then I want you to take my cock in your hand or mouth—any way—and finish me."

Luxen shuddered and pulled from Solo's grip, jerking away.

"Oh..." Solo's wings sagged. "Was it too much?"

Luxen hooked a hand around the back of his neck and kissed him hard, knowing words would fail him. Solo thrust the kiss back on him, his own desperation revealed in trembling muscles and wings. "You will never be too much or wrong," Luxen growled. He pulled Solo onto the bed with him, and while Solo fought to shuffle his trousers down, over his hips and thighs, Luxen found a bottle of lubricant in the nearby cabinet and returned to the bed to find Solo's peachy ass ripe and ready. Unable to resist, he did what he'd been wanting to do since Solo had paraded himself in front of the enclosure glass—he bent down, sucked on his ass cheek, and bit down. Solo yelped, his wings flew open, and then Solo laughed. Luxen chuckled, oiled his own cock, and without ceremony, eased a finger inside Solo's hole—cutting off his laugh.

"*Seraphim*," Solo puffed. "I don't..."

"It gets easier—better. Trust me. And let go."

"I do trust you. You have no idea how much."

That last sentence Solo had said so softly Luxen almost hadn't heard. "I'm beginning to," he whispered in return. He was desperate for this, Solo had made sure of it, going out of his mind for it, but he had to go slow. As hungry as Solo was, taking demon cock was not something that should be rushed, despite Luxen wishing he could ram into him, filling him to the brim.

He stretched the fine muscle, seeking the nub inside, and the moment he found it Solo's wings flared, each feather stretched. Solo moaned. "Ugh... yes, *that*."

Luxen couldn't help his own satisfied smile and didn't hide it when Solo glanced behind him.

"So smug?" Solo arched an eyebrow. "Stop teasing and get to the fucking."

Luxen laughed, hooked an arm under Solo, and drew him up so his back touched Luxen's chest; his feathers, where they overlapped near the shoulder joint, framed Luxen. "So demanding." Glorious red hair tumbled down his neck. Luxen coiled it in the fist of his right hand, while with his left, he stroked inside Solo's passage.

The mirror on the wall to his right displayed the stunning image of angel and demon, wings out, cocks eager. Their reflections were so painfully beautiful, Luxen had to look away. He didn't deserve this. "Look at us," he told Solo.

Solo turned his head. His whole body shuddered at the sight. He gasped, his face fraught with emotion. Amazement, but then sadness. Whatever that thought was that had made him sad, Luxen sought to banish it. He freed his hair, hugged him close, hooked an arm under his wing, skimmed his hip, and grasped his jutting cock. Now, Luxen had him, finger in deep and a hand on Solo's veined erection.

Solo moaned again and tilted his head back, resting it on the rise of his wing. "Yes."

Stretched wide, the muscles eased, Luxen withdrew his fingers and took himself in hand, then guided his length to Solo's tight, yielding hole.

"Yes," Solo moaned again. Luxen stroked him, felt his whole body tremble, locked in Luxen's arms, and when his ether crested, Luxen drove himself deep. Solo growled, then dropped forward onto his hands, wings fluttering back. Luxen gripped their arches, dick buried deep inside Solo's tight warmth, and figured he must have fallen into his own dreams, where anything was possible. Solo's ether boiled over, his passion freed, and Luxen was helpless to resist. All he could do was hold on and hope the dream lasted forever.

CHAPTER 22

Solo

Solo wasn't sure what he'd expected, but it hadn't been anything like the overwhelming, bone-melting pleasure riding him with every thrust of Luxen's cock. It felt good. Occasionally, the heavy pressure touched some part of him that stole his breath and made his heart stutter. Yes, this was what he craved: Luxen's grip on his wings, his cock buried deep, Solo's own member hard and leaking as it hung under him. His whole body blazed.

The rage he'd felt when he'd entered and seen what Luxen was watching dissipated, turned to mist, and burned off. It hadn't been a rage at Luxen, more at himself, for the shame that had rolled through him right after a savage wave of desire.

Now, though, there were no more thoughts, just feeling and knowing this was right. All too soon Luxen's rhythm spluttered, he swore and bucked, his thighs shuddering against the backs of Solo's. But before Solo could ask if he'd come, Luxen reached around, grasped Solo's cock, and began pumping ruthlessly. Solo's legs weakened under him. He couldn't form the words to ask him to slow, because he was about to—

He spilled hard, muscles spasming, cream soaking Luxen's fingers. He knew because their reflections showed it all in glorious candlelit softness. The image of them joined together branded itself into his memory so clearly it could never fade. Gold accents shimmered through Luxen's dark wings. They were both still half dressed, but it didn't matter. Solo saw everything he needed to.

Luxen freed Solo's wing, then slid from inside him. His fingers scooped between Solo's cheeks, sweeping up the glistening cream, and to Solo's delight, he licked his fingers clean. Oh Seraphim, it seemed everything Luxen did was designed to stop Solo's brain from working. He twisted, flung himself into Luxen's arms, and thrust a kiss on his lips that the demon lord had no chance of escaping. He tasted of cum and massage oil, whiskey, and Luxen. Solo swallowed it all down. Luxen rocked and fell back, wings splayed on the bed with Solo pinning him down. Solo grinned, nudged Luxen's nose with his own, and set free a contented purr, making Luxen chuckle. Luxen's hand came up, fingers coiled Solo's hair, then stroked.

He wanted to take this demon home, to his tiny house, and keep him forever. But there was the matter of Mikhail and Severn. Of a peace on the brink of war.

"No." Luxen used his thumb to pull the smile back onto Solo's mouth. "Whatever that thought is, unthink it. Your smile undoes me."

Solo slipped into the crook of Luxen's arm, his clothes askew, his wings heavy, but he'd never felt so thoroughly content before. "They said things about you..." He walked his fingers up Luxen's chest. "Things I didn't believe."

"What things?" Luxen's voice rumbled through Solo's entire body. He wanted to wriggle closer, tuck himself in and fold his wings over them both. Instead, he swirled his fingers around Luxen's shirt button, flicked it open, and dove his hand inside, absorbing the demon's innate heat.

Was there any point in telling Luxen things he already knew? How Konstantin and Mikhail would never absolve him? But he had to know, to guard against it. "They said you're the leader of a rebel cell intent on upsetting the peace. They wouldn't listen to reason—I tried to tell them they were wrong. They dismissed me."

"They thought I'd used my allure on you?"

"Exactly." Solo tilted his head up and saw Luxen's dark eyes peering down at him. He knew he hadn't used his allure. The same way he knew Luxen would never lead rebels against Mikhail and risk upsetting the peace they'd all fought for.

Luxen lifted his gaze to the ceiling and sighed. His fingers traced lazy circles over Solo's shoulder, where his shirt had slipped down. "Why are you here, Solo?"

"To warn you."

"You shouldn't have—"

Solo pushed against Luxen's chest, levering himself upright, and stared down at Luxen. In this moment, with them both sated, he had to say all the things he'd been thinking. There might not be another time. "You're not what they say. I know it. I feel it. I feel everything now, and I know you're good, you've changed. I fell hard for you. In every way. I left Aerie—"

"You *what?*"

"Well, technically, Mikhail kicked me out. I don't think I'm a general anymore. Or even an angel of Aerie."

Luxen's face almost looked panicked. "Solo—"

"No, listen. I have all these things inside. I need to get them out. They think I'm emotional or confused, or that I'm just addicted to your allure, but I've never seen things clearer than I do with you. For the first time in my life, everything makes sense. Instead of trying to be some impossible version of myself, I'm finally realizing I'm just me, and being me is enough. And part of that is listening to my heart and what it tells me... about you."

Luxen propped himself on his elbows. His face seemed pained, although Solo couldn't imagine why his words should hurt him. It was all good, wasn't it?

"You walked away from Mikhail *for me?*" Luxen asked.

"I know what you did to him—some of it. But you wouldn't do that again."

Luxen frowned. "How can you know that?"

Solo poked Luxen's chest, over his heart. "Because in there, there's a pup afraid of stars. And when the stars come for you, you do the only thing you can, you fight back. But if the stars don't come, you won't fight." It was so simple, so obvious; why couldn't everyone see it?

"You can't know that."

"Answer me this: Have you ever attacked first?"

"Some might argue my capturing Mikhail was an act of aggression."

"No, they're wrong. You saw an opportunity to weaken your enemy and you took it. Mikhail is not without blame.

Angels have too easily forgotten the terrible things they did—he did—during the war. So, have you ever attacked first?"

"I don't know... truthfully. Perhaps."

"You haven't. Your whole life you've defended yourself and other demons. You don't attack. You're backed into a corner and you react. The same as they're doing to you now."

Luxen bowed his head, eyes darting. Had he truly not realized this about himself?

"I'm right." Solo tipped his chin up and peered deep into his demon eyes.

"How did you get to be so wise, angel?"

He chuckled and flopped back into the crook of Luxen's arm. "It's easier to see the truth now I'm not living a lie."

"Mikhail is a fool to banish you. You're the only voice of reason in that place."

"Maybe. But if they won't listen, then there's no point being there."

Luxen stroked Solo's hair again and Solo sighed, relishing it.

"They are right about one thing," Luxen said. "I am the leader of a rebel cell."

Solo's heart stuttered. He pushed up on his arm again. "What?"

"It's not as it sounds. Samiel brought me in, believing I'd be the morale boost they need, and they accepted me. They have a plan to bring down Konstantin. For a while, I believed I could be a part of it, but it seems I no longer share their sentiment when it comes to angels."

"Then you're working against them?"

"I'm working to try and diffuse the situation, yes. They'll get themselves killed and risk upending the peace. Even I can see their cause is fruitless, and dangerous. As much as I despise Konstantin, I don't want to see a return to dead demons strewn across the killing fields. Nobody wins in war."

Warmth swelled in Solo's chest. He knew he'd been right about Luxen, but to hear it validated everything he'd been fighting for.

"Although, I'm surprised Djall is involved."

"Djall?" Solo asked, sitting up. "What's she got to do with it?"

Luxen propped his head on a hand. "As far as I can tell, she's rallying them. I haven't been able to get her alone to find out exactly what she's doing."

"Wait... Severn—Severn said they had someone trustworthy inside. It's her. It has to be. She's working for them, feeding them information on the rebels." Djall had clearly gotten it all wrong when it came to Luxen's involvement. "We need to get you and Djall in the same room together, tell her how it really is, how you're trying to help. She'll tell Mikhail. Maybe then they'll listen—"

"Solo, whatever I say, angels will never accept me, and perhaps they shouldn't. There is too much bad blood between us. Some things shouldn't be forgiven."

Solo didn't believe that. "Mikhail cut Severn's demonwings off and hung them on his wall. Severn has forgiven him. What could be worse than that?"

Luxen snorted. "Hardly the basis for a healthy relationship."

Relationship. Could he have one of those with Luxen?

His heart quickened. "So... what *is* the basis for a healthy relationship?"

"Not what they have." Luxen smirked. His expression softened when he saw Solo bite his own lip. "Respect," he said. Solo ticked that one off the list in his head. "Devotion. Commitment. Attraction, of course—not always physical." Check, check, check. Luxen's lips twitched around a smile. "They drive you crazy, you ask yourself why, but you love them anyway."

"You'd protect them, defend them, save them?"

"Yes. You know a lot for an angel who only recently learned he had feelings."

"I've been paying attention." Solo stroked Luxen's thigh. He had his trousers hitched up and undone, from their earlier adventures. Luxen had tucked his member away, but Solo could probably bring it to life again with a few touches. He only had to think about Luxen naked, his smooth muscular body, those mighty wings, and his own cock began to tingle.

Luxen stretched his arms behind him and laced his fingers behind his head. "If there were more angels like you, the war would have been over long ago."

"There *are* more like me."

"With cats?"

"Well, no."

"With an ex-High Lord to fuck?"

He blushed. "Probably not."

"With a heart made of gold and a dominating streak?"

Solo opened his mouth to deny it, but Luxen's warm smile cut him off, "Nobody is like you, Solo."

He liked the way Luxen looked at him now, with

hooded eyes and a lazy smile. As though Solo could straddle him, ride him deep, and Luxen would relish it. But it was more than the sex. He knew, without any doubt, Luxen would never hurt him. And he knew he had to protect Luxen, defend him, and save him from angels, from anyone who didn't understand him the way Solo did. Somehow.

Solo straddled Luxen's thighs and leaned over him. His hair spilled over Luxen's shoulder, pooling next to Luxen's head. Luxen's lips parted, dark eyes drinking him in. Solo considered taking his horns in his hands and kissing him silly, but he rather liked peering into the demon's gaze.

Luxen gathered his red locks and breathed them in, then fixed his gaze on Solo's eyes once more. "You are the only star I do not fear."

The door behind Solo slammed against the wall. He tried to lift his wing to see. Hands grabbed his ankle and dragged him from the bed. His chin struck the floor. Something hard and heavy pinned him down between his shoulders, then a hand came around and smothered his mouth. Growls bubbled around him. Shouts barreled back and forth. "Get his wings!" "Hold him!" "Harder! Don't let him—"

In a flash of silver feathers, an angel flew backward and struck the wall. He landed and lunged back onto the bed, where Luxen's magnificent demon wings flapped.

Solo blinked, trying to make sense of the chaos. The knee in his back dug deeper. He tried to throw out his wings, struck something, but then two great weights had hold of his feathers, driving his wing-arches closed. He bucked, tried to get a hand under him. They caught his arms and dragged them behind his back, binding them there.

"Open up, angel." A demon pinched his cheeks, driving his fingers between Solo's teeth so that he had no choice but to open his mouth. The slip of cloth went in and was yanked tight.

Silver wings.

Silver-winged *angel*. The witness who had claimed Luxen had been seen with an angelblade. The witness who had started all this.

Solo bucked and twisted. Hands grabbed him, shoved him back into Luxen's chair.

A blade pressed against his neck, its metal cold. A demon he'd never met before growled, "Stay!"

Gagged, head reeling, wings tied and trapped behind him, he panted hard and squinted through his hair at Luxen, who was held by two demons on the bed. But he hadn't been gagged. Blood wet his lips and chin, dribbling from his nose. He growled through clenched teeth. "Samiel!"

Sometime in all the chaos, Samiel had entered the room. He stood mere strides from Solo, his face lit with a triumphant grin. "What a disappointment you are, Luxen."

The silver-winged angel stood against the far wall, hands clasped in front of him, eyes cool and unemotive. Who was he? Why was he doing this? Solo tried to catch his eye, but he stared at Luxen.

Luxen fought, but the two demons flanking him were twice his size. "What is this?"

"I gave you a chance. I brought you home, and yet here you are." Samiel approached the bed. "In bed with an angel. Literally."

"Samiel, this is unnecessary. Let me go and we'll talk."

Samiel strode to the end of the bed. "I've listened to you talk for too long. No more talk."

Luxen slumped. He didn't look at Solo, just bared his teeth at Samiel. Solo tried again to meet the silver-winged angel's gaze. If he'd look up, he'd see Solo, see how wrong this was.

"The time has come for action," Samiel said. "And you're going to be the one to start the war."

"Why? What good will it do?" Luxen asked.

"What other way is there? This so-called peace where the angels lord it over us as though they've won? No. We are better than them, and we'll prove it."

"They'll kill you."

"Me?" Samiel laughed. "No. I'm not the bad guy here. You are. They'll kill you."

Luxen writhed again. "Whatever you have planned, I refuse to assist. More war is not the way."

"And to think I admired you." Samiel planted a booted foot on the end of the bed, leaning close to Luxen. "I followed your orders without question. And look where it got us."

"This is about Konstantin, not some righteous cause." Luxen glanced at the guards holding him, and the one holding Solo. "He's lying to you." His glare hung up on that angel, but the angel blinked slowly, immovable as marble. "Samiel's not doing any of this for demons. He wants revenge, nothing more."

"You're going to be our martyr, Luxen."

Luxen bared his teeth. "I'm not doing anything for you."

"No?" Samiel turned toward Solo. He marched closer. The demon was suddenly all Solo could see. Samiel plunged his hand into Solo's feathers, twisted his fist, and tore out a clump. Snapping darts of pain danced down Solo's wing. He cried out and writhed, trying to pull away from the pain.

Samiel threw the handful of feathers at Luxen's face. "You will do everything I say, or your feathered fuck-boy loses his fucking wings."

Luxen's gaze skipped to Solo. Luxen was good at hiding his emotions. But not here. Even Solo could see the panic on his face. Solo shook his head. Luxen couldn't do what Samiel wanted. Mikhail would kill him. If Luxen succeeded, they'd be right back where all this began, in the midst of war.

Luxen swallowed.

No! Solo mumbled through the rag. *Don't! Don't do this. Not for me. Don't restart a war.*

"Shut him up."

A backhanded whack threw Solo sideways. He hit the wall and slumped to his knees, ears ringing. Blood pooled around his tongue and soaked the rag. He gagged, spluttered, and swallowed as much as he could, almost choking.

"Don't touch him!" Luxen roared.

Samiel chuckled. "I told you," he said to the demons. "He'll do anything for a piece of angel ass. Just like Konstantin."

The demons in the room grumbled and snorted. Silver *finally* glared at Solo. He didn't laugh. None of this was amusing to him. Out of everyone in that room, Solo's gut told him Silver was the most dangerous. Why was he doing this? Solo shook his head again, but this time at the angel, hoping to get through to him. Silver lifted his head and turned his attention back to Samiel, unfazed.

"Today is a big day for the angels. They have some hotshot foreign angel arriving. Luxen, your task is simple. You'll fly into Aerie alongside Nathaniel here, as his prisoner, and when there, you will escape, attack, and kill Konstantin. Proof there can never be peace."

"You're insane," Luxen snarled. "I won't do it."

"Oh really?"

"The angels will hit back twice as hard. You'll kill more demons. This is madness!"

Samiel's snarl bubbled. "I listened to you and I lost everything. Now it's my turn to issue orders. You will do this or your fucking angel dies. Don't think I won't cut his pretty face." Samiel nodded at the demon holding Solo.

The demon looped Solo's hair around his hand and yanked, causing pain to blaze through Solo's scalp. A blade slashed through his hair, slicing it clean off, nicking his ear. Blood dribbled down his neck and the cool air whispered over it. The demon held up his trophy: a fist full of red hair.

Luxen roared and bucked. His wings snapped free, and for a few seconds, it seemed he might fight his way out. Then the blade was back at Solo's neck, and Luxen froze.

"Do as you're told," Samiel warned. "Kill Konstantin, and your angel lives. Refuse, and I'll cut him up, piece by piece, as you watch."

Luxen slumped between the demons again, breathless and trembling. "All right."

No! Solo pulled at his restraints. *No!* If Luxen went to Aerie, if he tried to hurt Konstantin, they'd kill him. He'd never see Luxen again. *Stop! Luxen, no!*

"Solo, it's fine," Luxen said. "My fate was inevitable."

No, no it wasn't. Solo was going to save him! Still could. If they'd all just listen!

"Let him up," Samiel said. The demons released Luxen.

Luxen climbed from the bed, rubbing his wrists. He vanished his wings and wiped the blood from his lip. "I do this, you'll let Solo go. Give me your word."

"You have it. He's of no use to me once you're done."

No—Seraphim, no. This wasn't right.

Luxen glanced over and Solo stilled, pleading with his eyes, begging him not to go.

"I'm sorry," he said.

Sorry? What? No. He couldn't do this! Solo loved him. He loved him as though he'd handed him half his heart and if he walked out of that door, Solo would never be complete again. Why... why couldn't he see that? Why didn't he know? If he left, it would break Solo open.

"No, don't go... I love you." But the gag garbled his words.

"Everything will be all right, Solo." Luxen turned away and the silver-winged angel fell into step behind him.

Then they were gone.

Tears brimmed in Solo's eyes. This pain... He'd never known anything like it. If an angelblade had cleaved him in two, it wouldn't have hurt as much. Oh, Seraphim... why? Why did he have to find love in one moment, only to have it taken away in the next?

Samiel threw a disgusted snarl at Solo's guard. "Keep him here until it's done."

CHAPTER 23

Luxen

Fat raindrops fell from London's heavy grey skies. Thunder grumbled some miles away. He usually loved to fly in thunderstorms. Not tonight. Tonight he wished his wings were lead.

"Can you fly in this?" the silver-winged angel, Nathaniel, asked, walking beside him. The same angel who had freed Samiel from the enclosure. The same angel who had fabricated seeing Luxen with an angelblade. Perhaps even the same angel who had told Mikhail and Konstantin that Luxen commanded the rebels.

"I'm demon. A little rain won't stop me." But it would stop Nathaniel if the rain fell in earnest.

Aerie's disks were out of sight behind the clouds. But Mikhail and Konstantin would be up there, having no idea fate was about to test them again. It hadn't been long ago that Luxen would have relished a second chance at bringing down Konstantin. If he hadn't met Solo, he still would thirst for the High Lord's death. Solo had made him see the world through a different lens. One of hope, instead of fear. "I do this and you'll report back to Samiel that it's done, and Solo can go free."

"Kill Konstantin and Solomon lives. I'll see to it myself."

"Somehow, I'm not reassured," Luxen drawled. He knew his enemies. He always saw them coming. He'd underestimated Samiel's mental state but until recently, Luxen had always had a plan, an angle, a play. But this angel... he hadn't seen him coming. Samiel had always been a follower, not a leader. Luxen suspected Nathaniel was behind everything, from the second he'd unlocked Samiel's door, to now, about to fly into Aerie to kill Konstantin.

Nathaniel was playing them all. He didn't look the type to plot a murder and start a war, but angels were deceptive in words and appearances.

"Ask," Nathaniel said. "You clearly want to."

"Why?"

The angel stopped on the sidewalk and flicked open his shining wings, giving them a few flaps to flick off excess water. "Because war is inevitable and false hope is cruel."

He sounded so like Luxen had. In fact, he saw himself in this angel. Cold, ruthless, shaped by war to survive. Nathaniel didn't yet have a Solo to save him. Some angels and demons might forever be lost. They couldn't all be saved. Understanding Nathaniel made Luxen's heart ache for Solo, for his passionate, funny, warm angel who didn't take anyone's shit, least of all Luxen's. Solo had to live.

"Come, demon." Nathaniel's wings beat the air. "Your fate awaits."

CHAPTER 24

Solo

DISTANT THUNDER RUMBLED, or that could have been Samiel growling as he paced at the foot of the bed. Samiel had left to see that Luxen and Nathaniel got on their way but had returned not long after. Solo tracked his every step, hoping the demon felt the weight of his glare.

Solo's tears had dried, crusting on his face. His wings no longer hurt. They'd mostly gone numb, still pinned behind him where he sat on the floor.

Samiel paced over his torn feathers and locks of cut hair.

Of all the emotions running through him since he'd been told he was allowed to feel, hate hadn't been one of them. Until now. It tasted like anger on his tongue, but more bitter. He'd been angry at Mikhail, at Severn; he'd been angry when he'd walked into this room and felt ashamed because the scene had aroused him. He'd been angry at himself for that. But he hadn't hated any of it.

This moment, now, with his wings tied, his mouth gagged, his hands bound—he hated now. Hated that he was too weak to get free, too weak to save Luxen. Hated that it had come to this. Everything was supposed to be better now, but for Solo, it had only gotten worse.

"Stop staring or I'll cut out your eyes," Samiel growled, still pacing.

Solo doubled down on the staring. If it bothered Samiel, then he'd stare two holes through his soul.

"What? Huh?" Samiel snarled. "Judging me. You think you're superior. That you have every right to own him. Luxen is—was a High Lord, and you fucked him like he was a piece of meat. You angels, you're all the same. It's all about you." Every step thumped the floorboards. He ranted some more about demons being used, how Luxen has used him to get to Konstantin, how he deserved to pay.

Solo mumbled around the gag.

Samiel pulled up short and glared down. "Everything was fine. We were at war. We had a reason, a purpose. It was honorable. We're demons, we live to fight. It's our lives. Konstantin took it from us for *his angel*."

Samiel was broken. Solo didn't even hate him, not really. He should. He could. But what was the point? Samiel was lost. He'd been lost for a long time. And Solo was sorry for that.

Samiel growled, knelt, and tore the gag from Solo's mouth, then shoved him backward, forcing his wings against to the wall. "Say it."

Solo wet his dry mouth and spat fluff and blood away. "Say what?" he croaked.

"How you hate me. How you want to kill me. Say it!"

"It would be a lie."

"Oh, fuck you, angel." He paced again. "Fuck you and your righteous sanctimony."

"I don't hate you." Solo shifted, trying to work his hands behind him to shake out the numbness. "But I think you're making a mistake."

"A mistake? I bet you do."

"Mikhail won't just retaliate, he will scorch demons from this earth. What you're doing... It will destroy everyone and everything. You're not fighting for what's right, or trying to save demons, you're killing us all."

"Mikhail can try."

"He did try before, and almost succeeded. You don't understand him, you don't understand love. He will raze London, and he won't stop there."

"He's not that unhinged."

"Not normally, no. But Severn is his whole world. If you..." Solo's voice caught, because somewhere deep down, he knew his words were true because he felt it too. "If you take Severn from him, it's over. All bets are off. You think your demons are safe in their territory? Think again. The pups recently born outside of war? He'll kill them. Anyone who crosses him, he'll kill them. Mikhail is wildfire. Only Severn can tame him."

Samiel narrowed his eyes, studying Solo. "It won't come to that."

Something dangerous fizzled inside Solo's chest. He wet his lips, tasting blood from earlier. "You don't understand. You don't know because you've never loved, have you?"

Samiel's laugh was cruel. "Love? An angel asks me about love? I have loved. Konstantin he... He was my first."

"No, he wasn't."

"Fuck you. What do you know?"

"I know if you'd ever loved him, you wouldn't do this. You wouldn't send Luxen to kill him because somewhere deep inside, you'd still love him, and you'd want to protect him, defend him, keep him safe. Because that's what love is, even if he doesn't love you back."

"Fucking angels." Samiel snorted. "Suddenly you know everything about love? You're so full of shit."

"You have to stop Luxen. You can catch up to them. You have to."

"Why? So you can suck Luxen's dick? There's more at stake here, angel, than you getting a concubi demon to suck you off."

The dangerous flicker inside grew brighter and hotter. "If you don't stop him, and he kills Konstantin for me, you'll set into motion the end of all things. It will happen again. The cycle of killing. Angels killed Seraphim for love. Luxen is about to kill Konstantin... for me." He choked on the words. "Please, Samiel. Please, I beg you. Don't let it happen again."

"All that shit... It's just angel fairytales to justify Mikhail's demon kink." He snorted, but there was some doubt in his side-eyed glance.

"It was real. You have the power to stop it from happening again."

Samiel backed up as far as the bed. "You're trying to get inside my head—"

"Samiel, listen—"

"No. I'm not listening to you. Konstantin has to die. Luxen has to die."

"For your revenge?"

"Yes!"

Fire ignited inside his chest. "What reason is that?! This is about you! Nothing else." The ropes holding his wrists creaked. His wings burned, muscles trembling. "At least tell me the truth, here and now. You're doing this for you. Admit it. You owe me that."

"Yes!" He growled. "They both need to die, and if it starts a war, I don't give a shit. Luxen betrayed me—betrayed his own kind, just like Konstantin."

The demon guard who had been standing at the door shifted restlessly. He glanced at Solo, and between them they shared a glimmer of understanding. This was wrong.

"I pity you," Solo said quietly.

"Fuck off." Samiel started forward. "Maybe I'll cut one of your wings off anyway, huh? It's not like he's going to know, seeing as Mikhail will kill him."

The demon at the door stepped forward. "Samiel—you gave your word."

"I said I'd let him go—not that I wouldn't rough him up a bit." Samiel's grin turned vicious and he approached Solo.

The fire that had been building within Solo scorched his veins, lighting him up from deep inside. He didn't know what it was or where it had come from, but it needed out. Hands clenched, he snapped the ropes holding his wrists, brought his arms around, and with a surge of fury, he thrust his wings apart, splitting the ropes holding them bound. Suddenly he was standing, wings spread, filling the room from floor to ceiling. Samiel reeled, off-balance. The guard's big arms wrapped Samiel from behind, and Solo landed a vicious right hook to Samiel's jaw that whipped his head back and slit his lip apart.

Samiel slumped in the guard's grip. Blood dribbled from between his lips.

The punishment wasn't enough for the crime, but it would have to do. He had to get to Luxen. Solo nodded at the guard. "Hold him. I'll send a flight down to retrieve him. Can you do that? *Will* you do that?"

The guard nodded back. "Yeah. Go."

Solo had a war to stop and a demon to save. He headed for the door.

"Love isn't worth it—*angel!*"

The warning in Samiel's voice turned Solo on his heel.

Samiel tore from the guard's grip in a surge of strength, grabbed his angelblade, and roared. Time slowed. Unarmed, Solo had no blade to parry with and no room to maneuver. He twisted, lifting his right wing at the last second, but Samiel's blade tore through his feathers. Fire sparked up Solo's wing and down into his shoulder. Didn't matter. He grabbed Samiel's exposed wrist and brought it down over his knee. Bone shattered. Samiel wailed, dropped the angelblade, and Solo's left hook knocked Samiel back.

Solo picked up the blade. It had been so long since he'd held one,; he'd never intended to again, wished he didn't have to now. But while the war was over, the battle clearly wasn't.

"You won't do it!" Samiel thrust out a hand. "You're too weak, too angel—" He must have seen his mistake on Solo's face because his own fell. "You're a fool. Luxen is demon. He'll *never* love you—"

Solo thrust the angelblade through Samiel's chest, deep into his heart, right to the hilt. Samiel gasped, choked, tried to push him back, but the fight soon drained out of him.

"Never underestimate an angel in love." Solo clutched the demon's jaw, making sure he saw into Solo's eyes. "I'd raze cities for him, that's how I know what I feel is real. This is my test."

He tore the blade free, backed up, and shook out his wings. Samiel clutched his chest, slid off the bed, onto the floor, and slumped there, eyes open, unmoving.

Perhaps Solo should feel sorry. Perhaps a better angel would. But all he felt was sad.

"Go," the demon grumbled. "Stop the war."

Solo fled the room, bloody blade leaving a dripping trail along the corridor behind him, and stumbled back through the rowdy bar. Someone said something, someone else tried to step into his path, to shove him, stop him. "Get out of my way!" Whether it was the bloody blade or his order, they stepped aside and a path opened for him, demons standing silent as he raced by.

He burst through the doors outside. Rain hammered against the ground in steel-like rods.

"No!" He couldn't fly in heavy rain. Not for long. No angel could. Water would soak him in seconds.

He flicked out his wings and bolted into a run.

Thunder grumbled.

Solo spread his wings, every feather, to their tips. Fire

lit up the right expanse, where the angelblade had torn through it. Didn't matter. Rain dripped from his feathers, soaked his hair and clothes. He flapped hard and launched skyward, carving through the waterfall of water. Lightning split the darkness. He had to get to Aerie; he had to stop the inevitable. He had to save him. Rain weighed him down, thrashed at him. The wind tried to beat him back. He pushed harder, fighting to climb, his wings growing heavier with every stroke. He could do this. He had to do this. This was his test. He wouldn't fail.

London vanished below in a swirl of dark. Darkness churned above too. Thunder rolled and boiled. Higher. He had to climb higher. His wings and shoulders burned, as though on fire. "Seraphim, help me... Help me save him."

Lightning cracked the sky, superheating the air, hissing too close to Solo's wet wings. Angels died in storms.

It didn't matter.

There was no time.

Failing wasn't an option.

He had to save Luxen.

CHAPTER 25

*L*uxen

AERIE WAS SO high in the clouds that every vast glass wall or open platform showed the churning storm. Aerie's lights fought off most of the dark, but occasionally a fork of lightning flashed, like a crack in Aerie's barriers. Thunder shook the floating city's pillar foundations. Nobody appeared to care—Nathaniel certainly didn't, marching beside him, his grip on Luxen's arm, guiding him along. If anyone asked why Luxen was here, he was to tell them he'd been caught and Nathaniel was bringing him to Mikhail. The plan seemed to be to walk Luxen right up to Konstantin when he wasn't expecting it and have Luxen stab him with Nathaniel's blade. So simple a pup could have thought of it, but hopefully a success, if Solo was to live.

It seemed destiny had always had this planned for him.

But Solo *would* live. The war, the demons, none of it mattered. He didn't care if angels and demons fought. Just that Solo survived. And perhaps that was selfish. So be it.

In Aerie's central atrium, hundreds of angels and demons had gathered around the main stage where Konstantin, Mikhail, and another angel stood. Mikhail spoke of peace and all they'd achieved.

Nathaniel picked his way through the crowd, going slow so as not to draw too much attention. A few strides from the stage, he slipped the blade into Luxen's hand. "When you're ready, High Lord."

The demons and angels around them gazed up at the stage. None noticed fate about to unravel around them.

Konstantin had his back turned to Luxen.

"Go," Nathaniel urged. "Before he sees you. Go, save your angel and kill Konstantin."

Yes. He had to do this. Even if he died in the next few minutes, struck down by what would surely be Mikhail's vengeance, Solo would be safe.

He reached the stage, climbed onto its edge, heard someone shout, "Angelblade!" Someone else called his name, although to try and stop him. A voice he knew.

Djall dropped out of the air. "Luxen, no. I can't let you do this." She loosed her whip. "Stay back."

"Too late."

Konstantin turned toward him, wings going wide and a snarl on his lips. The snarl quickly turned into a grin. "Let him try." He beckoned. "This has been coming for a long time, Lux."

"In that, we agree." *For Solo.* Luxen lunged.

CHAPTER 26

*S*olo

SOLO LANDED exhausted and wringing wet on Severn's balcony and threw open the doors, but the chamber was unlit and cold. Nobody was inside. *No, no, no...* There wasn't time to look all over Aerie for him. He'd be with Mikhail. Mikhail's chamber? It was quicker to fly but the storm still raged and Solo's wings trembled from overexertion. A horrible, bone-deep chill gnawed on his heart. He couldn't fly. Another sweep of his wings might be one too many.

Run. He had to run.

He bolted from the room, wet wings trailing behind him, the angelblade clutched in his trembling hand. Find Severn. Or Mikhail. Anyone who knew—

An angel! "Hey! Where's Konstantin!? Mikhail?!"

"General Solomon." The angel gasped. "Did you fly in that—?"

"Where are they?!"

"In the main atrium, giving a speech—"

Oh no. Of course that would be the place. In front of everyone. A thousand witnesses so none could dispute Luxen had drawn his blade. But nobody knew the truth. Nobody knew why.

He ran.

Everything hurt—his lungs, his chest, his heart, his wings. His every muscle screamed at him to quit. But he couldn't. This was his test. He couldn't fail it, not now. He had to save him.

He made it to the atrium. Countless angels and demons watched Luxen swing his blade for Severn. Swords clashed. He was too late.

"Why is nobody helping?" He shoved an angel aside. "Why aren't you stopping them?" He pushed at a demon. "Stop them! Somebody!"

"This is the demon way," another demon said.

"The what...?"

"Luxen struck first," an angel said.

A third demon added, "Konstantin has the right to combat—"

"Argh! He had no choice!" Solo shoved harder, trying to fight through the wall of bodies, but few budged, too engrossed in the sight of a far more powerful demon about to cut down one half his strength. It wasn't fair, it wasn't right.

"Stop!" Solo yelled. "He doesn't want—" He pushed through. Shoved. Elbowed. "He doesn't want this! Please... Someone..." Water dragged his wings down. Cold air filled his lungs, stole his breath, but he couldn't slow. He had to fight. Even if he was the only one left who would. That raging hot, boiling mass he'd felt earlier overspilled, and with a roar, Solo thrust his wings over the heads of everyone there and tore into the air. He came down hard on the stage, landing on his knee between Luxen and Severn, instantly blocking them, knocking both back. "Stop this *now!*"

"Solo?" Luxen panted. "Solo, what—" Luxen's sword hand dropped to his side.

Solo flung a hand back, holding Luxen there. This wasn't over. "Don't move." Djall stood behind him, her dagger raised, poised to stab Luxen between his wings. "Nobody *fucking* move." He snarled at Severn. "That includes *you*."

"Solo," Severn barked. "Get out of the way."

It hurt to breathe. Everything was broken. His heart, his wings, all of him. But damn them, he wasn't ever going to stop fighting for what was right. "Seraphim help me, I will raze this damned birdcage to the ground if you do not listen to me!"

Mikhail hung back, and behind him stood a female angel who had to be the Guardian everyone was so desperate to impress. Well, she was definitely going to see *something impressive*.

"This is demon business." Severn straightened. "Luxen came here to kill me. This is my right—"

"Shut up." Solo thrust his blade toward Severn. "I warned him and I'm warning you. Do not test me."

Severn growled. It had been a long time since they'd clashed like this, but if Severn would not back down, then Solo would fight him. "Luxen manipulated you," Severn said. "He drugged Mikhail. He's a cheat and a snake. I can't let him live. He *must* die."

"No."

"What?"

"No. He doesn't die here. And yes. You can let him live. If you so much as raise that blade against him, then Seraphim help me, you will have to cut me down."

"You're allured," Severn snarled, disgusted.

Solo thrust with his blade. Severn parried, swinging down, and Solo jabbed, driving Severn back. And for a few seconds, they clashed, blades ringing, Solo pushing. He couldn't stop Severn, not wrecked as he was. But he'd damn well die trying.

Solo stumbled, and Severn stopped swinging when he could have cut Solo down. "Touch him and I will kill you, Severn. Is that clear enough for you? Do you hear me?" Solo panted. "I'm not allured. My head has never been clearer. You said my test would come. It has, and this is it. I will fight every angel and demon here to save Luxen. Seraphim as my witness, I vow this now." The room spun, the air suddenly thick, but he had to hold on. They had to know. They had to listen. "He didn't want this. He was sent here by Samiel to kill you or I'd be killed. He had no choice. He was doing this to *save me*."

Severn growled, but Mikhail's hand came down on the demon's shoulder. "Wait. Hear Solo out."

Tears blurred Solo's vision. His wings burned so much they might shatter at any moment. Gods, he had to make them see how much Luxen had changed, how he deserved to be among them.

Severn lowered his blade. "Luxen was working with the rebels—"

"To stop them." Solo sighed or shuddered, he wasn't even sure anymore. "To save demon lives, but you all think he's a lost cause. He was right, that's all you ever want to see. He's not what you think. He's fierce and brave. He doesn't want war any more than we do." He couldn't stand any longer and dropped to his knees. His wings sagged, too heavy, too wet, too cold. Gods, he had to hold on. He had to make them see.

Severn stepped forward. Solo raised his blade again, even as it wobbled in his hand. "Don't—don't hurt him."

His body finally surrendered to the darkness, and he fell, hoping—wishing he'd done enough.

CHAPTER 27

*L*uxen

Solo lay still at Konstantin's feet. Nobody was moving to help him. With a growl, Luxen threw his blade down and dashed to Solo's side, but steel touched his neck before he could get there, jerking him to a halt. At the blade's end, Konstantin glared. "You don't touch him."

"Did you hear nothing he said?" Luxen snapped, then backhanded the blade aside and dropped to his knees. He brushed Solo's chopped hair from his face. His skin was ice against his palm. "He's cold." Luxen spread his wing over Solo's wet, motionless body. Sodden feathers clung to Luxen's dry wing-membrane.

He bent low, bundling him closer. Warmth. He needed to get Solo warm. "So cold…" Could Solo die from this? No, Luxen's heart couldn't stand it if these were Solo's final moments, spent trying to save a nothing demon like him.

"Aerius, please," he whispered to the demon god, wherever they may be, if they were even real. Solo was strong. Stronger than Luxen. He'd live. He had to.

"His wing," Djall said. "He's bleeding. Healers! Quickly!"

Luxen sensed Mikhail first—his formidable presence like that of a rising tide or the boiling storm outside. With Solo's head cradled in his lap, Luxen met Mikhail's knowing gaze. All that had passed between them before now, he regretted it. Had there never been a war, had the lies been lifted long ago, their lives might have been very different. But they had been mortal enemies, and now all Luxen could do was hope Mikhail had it in him to forgive.

Mikhail reached down and touched Solo's slick forehead.

"Take him to the healers," Konstantin ordered.

"No," Mikhail said. "He stays here. He's exactly where he needs to be." Mikhail nodded and Luxen folded himself over Solo's prone body, bringing his wings around to warm them both and keep out anything that would hurt him.

"It will be all right," Luxen whispered, stroking Solo's hair. "I promised you that, and I meant it. Everything is going to be all right, Solo."

Solo had come for him.

He'd gotten free of Samiel, flown through a deadly storm, and stopped Konstantin. All for Luxen. He'd saved him.

Nobody had ever done anything like that for Luxen. Nobody had ever cared enough to try. He'd always been alone, fought tooth and claw alone, lived alone.

"Find Samiel," Konstantin grumbled, his voice moving farther away.

Samiel was dead. Luxen knew it. Solo could withstand a great deal, but he had a breaking point. Luxen tucked him closer still, breathing in his wet meadow scent. He couldn't look at his wings. He didn't want to see how bent and battered they were.

A hand touched Luxen's back, offering comfort.

Mikhail.

Then he, too, was gone.

He didn't know if they'd all gone, or if they stayed nearby and waited. None of them mattered. Only one soul in all the world mattered. He listened to Solo's soft breathing, his strong heart, and he kept him close, so close—as though they were one.

Hours passed. Solo's shivering faded. Sometimes voices drifted over them. But Luxen kept them out, kept his wings locked and Solo safe inside. Until his breathing evened, and his heart thumped loud and strong.

"Hey..." Solo's pale hand touched Luxen's arm, then his face. And his green eyes blazed. "You okay?"

Luxen's croak of a laugh sounded a lot like a sob. "You scared me, angel." He tucked a loop of ragged hair behind Solo's ear.

"Sorry?"

Gods, this angel. Luxen kissed his forehead. "Thank you."

"Oh." He swallowed. "It worked then? I wasn't sure if I could stop... them"

"You did." Luxen stroked his face. So soft. So fierce. "You stopped it all." He lifted his wings off, letting a crack of light spill in, then raised them high behind him so Solo could see he was home, in Aerie, right where he'd fallen. But they weren't alone.

Solo propped himself up on an arm, and Luxen squinted into the light. Angel and demon wings encircled them, shielding them. One by one, they fluttered closed, and the wall they'd created came undone, wing by wing.

Solo's small hand found Luxen's and held tight. Luxen squeezed back.

Mikhail's wings had been among the many keeping them safe. He withdrew with the rest, dipping his chin in acknowledgement.

"Did he just... Is Mikhail okay with *this*?" Solo asked.

"Yes."

Angels and demons left, until there was just one left standing in the atrium. Konstantin. "We found Samiel," the High Lord said, face guarded and arms crossed.

Solo's hand tightened some more.

Luxen closed his eyes. Solo hadn't wanted *that*. And neither had Luxen. But not every demon could be saved.

Konstantin nodded. Nothing else needed to be said. He breathed in, wing-tips lifting. "Oh, and Solo... I swear your cats multiply every time I feed them. You need to get down there, when you're ready. "

"Is Five back?"

"I have no idea. They all look the same. Maybe Luxen can help find the missing one?" He arched an eyebrow at Luxen, questioning him with that one gesture, then apparently satisfied with events, he stalked off.

Luxen didn't feel inclined to move. If he moved, whatever this was that was happening might break apart and fall away. "Is this real?" he whispered, mostly to himself. He was in Aerie. Angels and demons had stood with him as he'd held Solo close.

Solo stumbled to his feet, dragging Luxen with him,

and cracked opened his stiff wings. Red feathers stuck out at odd angles. Some had fallen away. His hair was a ragged, hacked-at mess, but his freckles still glowed like tiny stars on his face. Luxen had to fight his instincts not to drag him into his arms and devour him in a kiss.

"Hm, demon. Before we go home, I need your help with these wings." Solo stretched his right wing and another feather seesawed away. "Do you preen?"

"Do I preen?" Luxen echoed. Such an angel thing to ask. "I can try."

Solo's smile tilted, color touched his cheeks. "It involves you getting extremely close and very personal with these." His wings stretched wider.

Luxen swallowed and hauled Solo into his arms. "Just so long as I'm with you."

CHAPTER 28

*S*olo

LUXEN PREENED VERY WELL, and then with his hands already all over him, it seemed like such a waste not to explore some more of the sex. It was different this time. Not the fucking. Solo was beginning to understand how the sex was a language he was only now learning. Luxen was a good teacher.

Still weak from fighting the storm, he lay back on the bed in his chamber and relished Luxen's touch, his mouth, his fingers stroking, and how his big, deep eyes devoured the sight of every inch of Solo. He may have fallen asleep with Luxen stroking his thigh and woken again tucked against the demon's warm side.

Luxen dozed, and Solo listened to his thumping heart while trying to shake the image of Luxen striking at Severn—his mission hopeless, but his face determined. He might just have won from will alone. Severn had underestimated him. Gotten him all wrong. Everyone had. But they were learning. They were listening. That had to be a good thing.

Besides, they'd learned if anyone touched Solo's demon, they'd have Solo to contend with.

Luxen came around, his voice all gruff and grumbly. He plucked a fallen red feather from his impressive chest and twirled it between his fingers. "Demon wings require a great deal less maintenance."

Solo sat up and flicked his fingers along the loose membrane he'd been sleeping on, making Luxen gasp. "And are a lot more sensitive."

The demon growled and pounced, pinning Solo to the bed, then dug his fingers into Solo's hips. Laughter sprung out of him. "No!" he wailed. "Tickle me and die!"

Luxen chuckled and eased off. He climbed from the bed, gloriously naked, and stretched in the sunlight pouring in through the balcony doors. His dark wings twitched and flicked out behind him, so he took up almost an entire side of the chamber. Solo let his gaze travel down his back to his ass and rolled onto his side, propping his head on his hand. He might never get enough of seeing Luxen naked.

"Hm, keep staring and I'll have no choice but to devour you cock first."

A little thrill tickled through him. "I'm up for the sex."

Luxen laughed and bent to pick up his shirt. "It's just sex, Solo. Not *the* sex."

"It's *never* just sex."

He chuckled again and peered over his shoulder. "You're right. It never is. Not with you."

"How many people have you had the sex with?"

Luxen buttoned up his shirt. "I'm concubi. How many dinners have you eaten?"

Then the answer was *a lot*. He liked the idea of watching Luxen with others, but not Luxen doing those things without Solo with him. He didn't like *that* idea at all.

"Does it bother you?" Luxen asked, eyebrow raised.

"I don't know." He rubbed at his chest, trying to rub away a strange ache. "Yes, I think it does."

Luxen rested his ass on the edge of the bed. "With you, I don't need anyone else. You are a feast in all ways." He trailed his fingers down Solo's hip, threatening to make him laugh and writhe all over again. Luxen leaned in, so close to a kiss that Solo tilted his head and lost himself in Luxen's gaze. "Unless you want to see me with another?"

Solo's heart gave a lusty flutter. "Is that wrong, to want that?"

"Never."

"Maybe, then." He chewed his lip. "I want to try."

"We'll explore what you like and dislike. We have all the time."

Luxen really was a good teacher, but what if he grew bored of Solo? What if Solo wasn't enough? He didn't pretend to know much about the sex, whereas Luxen lived it. He'd said the threesomes were *his life*. Everything was happening so fast. What if, when the storm clouds lifted and the dust settled, Luxen walked away? Samiel had said Luxen might never love him...

"Will you stay with me?" He hadn't meant for the question to sound so small when it meant so much, but he'd been afraid to ask it.

"Do you want me to?"

"Yes."

"Good. Because I almost started a war for you. I'm not going anywhere." Luxen's big hand caught Solo's chin. "I mean it. You vowed to protect me and I vow this now: I'm yours, for however long you want or need me. My life was a shadow before. You light me up, Solo, in ways I didn't know were possible."

"Oh." His heard thudded. It was no small thing to have a demon vow such things. It seemed that perhaps this spark they had together might be long-lasting. He wanted that. He wanted it a lot. He'd been alone for so long... "Come home with me."

"To your family of felines?" Luxen grinned, then slammed a kiss on Solo's mouth and mumbled, "I'm ready when you are."

∽

THE CATS MEWED and purred and dashed between Solo's feet. They'd missed him, which was nice. Or maybe they just didn't like Severn as much. That was also possible.

"There are so many..." Luxen tripped over one in the tiny house's corridor.

"Just six... well, five now I suppose. Five left."

"Five cats left?"

"She's called Five. I don't know what happened to her."

Solo made sure they were all fed. Luxen changed their water, his expression content as One *prrped* and rubbed against his leg. One was a good judge of character. Solo set the fire in the front room fireplace, warming the house through, and after returning from letting the cats outside, he found Luxen sprawled in one of the big armchairs, two cats curled in his lap and another draped over the back of the chair behind him.

He shrugged gently, so as not to disturb them. "It appears I'm theirs now."

Solo leaned against the doorframe and folded his arms, taking in the sight of the formidable demon being used as a bed for tiny felines. He couldn't blame them; Luxen was always warm. Solo might even be a little jealous.

A knock sounded at the door. Chuckling, Solo answered it to find Severn waiting in the early evening light. "If you've come here to tell me I'm allured, then—"

"I came to apologize."

Solo narrowed his eyes and waited.

"Right." Severn cleared his throat. "I'm sorry, I was wrong. To be fair, Luxen and me... There's *a lot going on* there. I'm never going to forgive him for the shit he did, but..."

"But?"

Severn fidgeted on the step and sighed. "I can not try and kill him every time I see him?"

It was a start. And he did appear genuinely sorry.

"But if he hurts you I will pull his wings off and beat him—"

"I can hear you," Luxen grumbled from the front room.

Severn pressed his mouth closed, then said loud enough for Luxen to hear, "Sentiment still stands."

"Noted," Luxen called back.

"He's kinda tied up," Solo said.

Severn's lips twitched. "Literally?"

"No..." Although, that did sound like something they

might explore in the bedroom later. "The cats have claimed him as theirs."

Severn laughed. "That's something I never thought I'd hear. Hey, did you find Five?"

"No, I think she's gone for good."

"She'll come back." Severn smiled, but his smile soon faded. "Listen... Nathaniel, the angel you told me about, the one who orchestrated this clusterfuck? We know where he is. Mikhail said not to tell you, as it would *ruin the mood,* apparently." He did a good impression of Mikhail's lofty voice. "But Solo, do you want in? You can come with me to secure him."

Luxen emerged from the front room and stopped beside Solo. His trousers were patchy with cat fluff, but he didn't seem to care. "What's Nathaniel's sentencing?"

Severn's easy mood chilled now that Luxen was present. "Undecided."

"Let me talk with him."

"You?" Severn glanced at Solo. Solo raised his eyebrows. This would be a good time for Severn to prove he was sorry.

"He and I have a lot in common," Luxen said.

Severn poked his tongue into his cheek, clearly refraining from saying something derogatory due to Solo's presence.

"You have a lot in common with the angel who manipulated you and Samiel in an effort to restart the war? Is that what you're telling me, Lux?"

"You either trust me or you don't, High Lord."

Severn's cheek twitched. "Solo trusts you. And I trust him, so... Fine. Talk to Nathaniel. But we must go now. I'm charged with his arrest before morning. And if you spook him, or give him the heads-up, it'll be Solo you answer to."

Luxen checked Solo, his gaze questioning, and Solo nodded. Solo watched Luxen descend the steps. Severn eyed him as though he was a wild animal about to attack. Maybe he should go with them to keep the peace? But he trusted Luxen in this. He wouldn't do anything to jeopardize how far they'd all come. Although... Severn had a tendency to lash out when riled—

"It's fine," Luxen said, reading Solo's face. "Isn't it, Konstantin?"

"Yeah. We'll be fucking fine," Severn grouched.

It was not fine—Solo nodded and closed the door—but hopefully it would be.

CHAPTER 29

*L*uxen

"He's too good for you," Konstantin growled, walking alongside Luxen to a point on the street where they had room to spread their wings and get air-bound.

"Oh, I know."

"If you break his heart I will break your face, then your wings, then your legs."

So predictable. "I appreciate your concern."

"It's not concern for you. Solo is honorable, brave, thoughtful, caring, and the most bad-ass angel I know. If you so much as pluck a feather from his wing, it won't just be me coming down on you, it'll be Mikhail, and we both know you don't want his wrath on your back."

By the gods, when would the threats end? "Are you finished?"

Severn snarled. "Not by a long shot."

"Yes, you are." Luxen stopped mid-street and faced Konstantin. "One, he doesn't need you to fight his battles for him. He's more than capable of fighting his own. Two, respect his choices, or for all your bluster, you don't respect him. Three, if you are still so hung up in your own head that you haven't heard or seen any of what's happened, I love him. I believe—hope—he loves me, although you and I at least agree I am not worthy, but I'm trying to be." He'd said it all in one long beat, and now done, he took a breath and stepped back. When Konstantin's glower didn't turn into violence, he added, "So unless you have anything to add, I suggest we find Nathaniel before he flees London." Luxen took to the skies and within seconds, he heard Konstantin's wingbeats behind him. A glance back revealed the High Lord smiling. Perhaps Konstantin—or Severn, as he preferred—wasn't a lost cause, after all.

※

NATHANIEL, the silver-winged angel, sat alone on a bench overlooking London's old docklands, not far from where countless angelblades glittered in the ground, left there as a reminder of war and the countless dead who had paid for peace with their lives.

Luxen landed several meters away, so as not to spook him, and walked the edge of the dockside. The Thames's inky black waters lapped at the dock below. Above, stars winked down on a quiet London. Luxen didn't fear them as he used to, but opens skies and clears nights did still chill him. Maybe, one day soon, now they had peace, he'd appreciate the night sky without looking for threats.

Nathaniel couldn't have failed to see him, but he didn't acknowledge his approach, just stared across the Thames into the stillness of the killing fields.

Luxen stopped alongside him and waited a while, soaking up the quiet atmosphere. "What happened to you?"

Nathaniel leaned forward, rested his elbows on his knees, and bowed his head. "I think you know."

Luxen cast his gaze from the angel, across the nothingland. He could guess. Nathaniel had lost someone. Someone he'd cared for. They'd all lost others, family, friends, lovers. Nathaniel had lost someone close, and it had broken him. He didn't have an ancient prophecy playing out to seal his fate. He was one angel among many, scarred by a grief he was only now allowed to feel.

If Solo were here, he'd know what to say. He always did.

"I don't pretend to know what our future holds," Luxen said. "I'm only now realizing I have one. But..." He gazed up, at the stars. "I do know the pain fades, if we let it. Clinging to it... Over time, it makes it worse."

Nathaniel swallowed. "So how do I let it go?"

"One day at a time."

Nathaniel lifted his gaze. His angel eyes shone with unshed tears. Luxen had killed hundreds like him. Sent demons to kill more. He might have been the one to issue the order to kill Nathaniel's love, and by the gods, he was sorry for his part in it. They couldn't ever go back to war. Nathaniel was perhaps learning that.

"I saw him, Solomon—saw him stand against the impossible for you. He's remarkable," Nathaniel said.

"Yes. He is."

"I wasn't the only one who saw him. He stood up, he defended you, to the very end. He's one of us. Just an angel. But he changed hearts and minds in that moment."

Pride swelled in Luxen's chest. "There are more like him. Like you."

Nathaniel snorted. "I think my time might be up. Are they coming for me?"

"Yes."

He nodded. "I won't run from my fate."

"I'm not sure we can," Luxen said, thinking of Solo and how, by some miracle, they might have a chance together despite the odds stacked against them.

Demon wings blocked out the stars—Severn spiraling downward. Several angels tagged along behind him.

Nathaniel got to his feet and clamped his wings closed, signaling he had no intention of fleeing. "You don't hate me for what I did?"

"An angel taught me how hate is mostly destructive."

"I can guess which angel. Only *mostly*?"

"He's a lot nicer than I am. And I'm still learning."

Severn landed with his angels and Nathaniel went to one knee, offering up his wrists. "Forgive me, High Lord, Your Grace. I accept my fate and your punishment, as you see fit."

Severn arched an eyebrow at Luxen and ordered the angels to bind Nathaniel, then for them to fly with him back toward Aerie.

Severn remained on the dockside with Luxen. The sounds of lapping water and the distant hum of London traffic filled the air.

After a few minutes, Severn said, "Aerius told me to

forgive you. They were half-insane, but they also knew their shit."

Luxen arched an eyebrow. Aerius had mentioned him? He'd featured in the demon god's thoughts? That was news to Luxen. "I'm sorry for what I did to you and Mikhail."

"Yeah, I think you are." Severn turned his head and frowned at Luxen. He could just as easily be thinking about shoving Luxen into the Thames as he could be thinking of forgiving him. "You're still a dick, though. That's never gonna change."

"Probably not."

Severn laughed, flapped his wings, and lifted into the air. "Go back to Solo before he comes looking. Oh, and some advice. Don't ever get on his bad side. Solo will cut you as soon as kiss you."

"I am aware."

Severn left, laughing to himself, or perhaps at Luxen. Only time would tell. Time he now had, thanks to Solomon, Angel of Aerie, Luxen's angel, the one star he'd grown to love.

CHAPTER 30

Solo

HE'D SELFISHLY SPENT most of the night wrapped in Luxen's wings and limbs. Solo hadn't asked what had happened with Nathaniel. Luxen's smile when he'd returned was enough to know everything was going to be all right, and then he'd scooped Solo off his feet and against a wall...

Early the next morning, Solo padded, near naked, to the kitchen and set about brewing some coffee—a drink the humans seemed to adore but had little effect on Solo. He planned to make a pot for Luxen. It seemed like a suitable morning task to do.

"Solo?" Luxen called. "Get up here..."

The quiver in Luxen's voice triggered Solo's sprint. He bounded up the stairs. Luxen wasn't in their room. "Where—"

The demon sat on the bed in the spare room, his wings open, his back to the door.

"What's wrong? What happened?" Solo almost reached for the non-existent blade at his side. Whatever it was, they'd tackle it together. Anything. He'd protect Luxen forever.

Luxen bent down and slowly cracked open the bedside cupboard.

Solo leaned over his shoulder, held on to his wing arch, and peered down at the puddle of floof inside the cupboard. "What is that?"

"I think, Solo, Five has become four more."

"She what?"

The puddle of floof moved, and two tiny ears pricked upright. A tiny cat mewed. And now he'd seen one, he saw the rest curled up against mom. Four fluffy muffins. Kittens! "Oh."

"You know what this means?" Luxen asked.

Solo's heart fluttered. Was it bad? Would Luxen ask him to get rid of them? What if he made him choose between him and the cats?

Luxen smiled and dropped his wing, sliding Solo close enough to kiss. "We're going to need a bigger house."

ALSO BY ARIANA NASH

Please sign up to Ariana's newsletter so you don't miss all the news & get a free short story.

www.ariananashbooks.com

Also by Ariana Nash

Silk & Steel Series

When Eroan, one of the last elf assassins, is captured trying to kill the dragon queen, he knows his death is imminent. Until the queen's youngest son, Prince Lysander, inexplicably lets him go.

Eroan expected death, but in the darkest of places, when all hope is lost, love finds him instead.

This epic fantasy adventure topped the Amazon charts for months. Discover the darkly delicious world of Silk & Steel today.

Click here to start the adventure with Silk & Steel, Silk & Steel #1

∽

Prince's Assassin Trilogy
(now complete!)

Soldier, Nikolas Yazdan, survived a brutal eight year war, but can he survive the wicked and cruel Prince Vasili Caville and the lies within the Caville palace?

Read King of the Dark, Prince's Assassin #1, today to find out!

∽

ABOUT THE AUTHOR

Born to wolves, Rainbow Award winner Ariana Nash only ventures from the Cornish moors when the moon is fat and the night alive with myths and legends. She captures those myths in glass jars and returning home, weaves them into stories filled with forbidden desires, fantasy realms, and wicked delights.

Sign up to her newsletter and get a free ebook here: https://www.subscribepage.com/silk-steel

Printed in Great Britain
by Amazon